PRAISE FOR ROBERT'S WORK

Chute sucks you in from word one and pulls you down his post-apocalyptic rabbit hole! You will sleep with the lights on, covers pulled over your head, and dust off the old teddy bear for comfort. Chazz ranks among the top tier of our generation's storytellers. ~ Alex Kimmell, Author of *The Key to Everything*

Robert Chazz Chute is such a skilled spinner of tales that the reader is more than willing to suspend any possible disbelief to go along for the ride. ~ David Pandolfe, author of *Jump When Ready*

It's not very often one finds a writer with such a dark side that has such a great sense of humor. ~ Glenn Roberts, Amazon reviewer

The author has a definite talent with words and ideas. ~ Love to Read!, Amazon reviewer

His words lift and dance off the page, bringing the story to life. ~ Kindle Customer, Amazon reviewer

The world-building is horrifically well done with twists and turns and deceit around every corner. ~ Wanda, Amazon reviewer

RCC blends characters' beliefs & worries concerning society's failures, plus vivid action scenes skillfully. ~ RMerkl, Amazon Reviewer

Nothing but sheer exhaustion could tear my eyes from the captivating dance of words choreographed by Robert Chazz Chute. ~ Halph Staph, Amazon reviewer

Wonderful action constantly holds your interest. ~ Sharon Finn, Amazon reviewer

The complexity and attention to detail throughout absolutely blow me away. ~ Kindle customer, Amazon Reviewer

Very few authors impress me with their actual writing style, it's usually always about the story. But this author paints such beautiful vivid pictures with words that I found myself not only enjoying the story but enjoying the way the words created images in my mind. I know that sounds corny, but it is true. ~ B.H., Amazon reviewer

Chute gives us a story worthy of Stephen King. A read both thoughtful and fun. ~ Linda Beer Johnson, Amazon reviewer

The author does an excellent job building the characters and getting you invested and involved. ~ Michele L. Hebert, Amazon reviewer

I just can't say in words what a powerful author this is! ~ Delinda L. Calkins, Amazon reviewer

Robert Chazz Chute writes so skillfully as to make the supernatural seem perfectly logical - and terrifying! There are twists, turns, and surprises galore. You will be glad you bought this book - until you lose sleep because you can't put it down. ~ johligo, Amazon reviewer

When I want to read apocalyptic books or zombie stories, those books have to also be extremely well written and something that I could recommend with zeal and confidence to everyone I know. Robert Chazz Chute's books are exactly that. ~ Mazie Lane, Amazon reviewer

He makes the stuff that is obviously fiction, believable. ~ W. Nickels, Amazon reviewer

I am a lover of paranormal, dystopian novels and depth of story as well as intelligence in writing style, and Robert has it all. Humor, wit, depth, intelligence, and an awesome way with words/writing. ~ Amazon Customer, Amazon reviewer

OUR ZOMBIE HOURS

ROBERT CHAZZ CHUTE

Licensing Notes

Our Zombie Hours

ISBN (ebook) 978-1-927607-80-0
ISBN (paperback) 978-1-927607-79-4

INTRODUCTION

During the global pandemic, I hid in my blanket fort and poked away at my big book, the one I hope will become an instant apocalyptic classic. After nearly two years of writing *Endemic*, it was almost ready for publication. However, due to COVID, there was an unexpected delay in my editorial pipeline. Couldn't be helped.

Something good happened, though. I got my writing mojo back. I suddenly couldn't wait to write more. As Halloween approached, I thought, how about I come up with a quick read for zombie fans?

In many of my books, I've played with the tropes of the genre. In *This Plague of Days*, some zombies evolve to become sentient. (What's a sentient zombie, you ask? That's a vampire.) In *AFTER Life*, nanotechnology has its way with humans and zombies alike. In *Endemic* (soon to be released as I write this), the infected are zombie-adjacent. It was time to do something pretty much tried and true for the purists.

Most of the afflicted in this anthology are closer to the expected tropes of the genre. I bend some rules here and there, but some horror fans ("true horror fans?") need zombie fiction closer to what they expect. Still room for surprises, though. That's the fun of it.

Enjoy *Our Zombie Hours*, and celebrate Halloween all year if you want.

Cheers and all the best!

~ RCC

ACKNOWLEDGMENTS

Thanks to my editorial team. Editrix Supreme Gari Strawn of strawnediting.com and beta reader Russ Sawatsky are always on point.

My writing career would be dead in the water if not for all the love and support from Janice AKA She Who Must Be Obeyed. Thanks Boo.

For all those who enjoy quick hits of horror and want Halloween to last all year long.

ILLUSIONS AND DELUSIONS

Jayden drove me to the Las Vegas suburbs in his whisper-quiet Prius, and there was not a zombie in sight. As he drove, he told me what a hero I was about to become. "Nate, it's going to be easy. We've hardly seen a single predator in weeks."

"Maybe that's because the people doing our supply runs don't dare to go farther into the city," I replied. "The cannibals are sticking close to their food source. They're rabid and we should stay away from them."

Jayden beamed a toothy grin to reassure me. I told him to keep his eyes on the road. "If you barrel into one of these abandoned vehicles, it's a long walk back for both of us. You know, assuming we survive."

He was quiet for a few minutes before he tried again. Finally, he said, "Everybody gets a turn at this job. Think of how Cheryl is going to look at you when you lure them into the trap for us. You'll have everyone's respect, man!"

"Have I lost anyone's respect?"

His answer was a careless shrug.

I'd seen how he looked at my girlfriend. Cheryl seemed to enjoy his attention, too. When I asked her about that, she laughed it off. "He's just a flirt and so am I. That's how I got you."

"You do have me. Does he know that?"

She took a little too long to answer before she said, "Sure."

The deeper we went into the suburbs, the more I suspected Jayden didn't want me to succeed in the mission. Before Jayden joined the group, I never worried about being perceived as a coward. But, of course, I was scared. If I didn't make it back to camp, he'd have Cheryl to himself.

Weaving past abandoned cars, Jayden told me, "We can't stay out on the edge of the city forever. We weren't meant to live in the desert."

"Live? Maybe not. It's how we've survived, though. Haven't enough people died? We can do supply runs into the city, stick together, work together, and — "

"Our people are exhausted," he said.

Until a month before, Jayden had been a stranger, and our little band of survivors had been my people. It was as if he'd moved in and taken over without the courtesy to tell me I was fired.

"We can't live in an RV park forever, circling the wagons as if we're pioneers in the Old West, always terrified of the next raiding party. The grind and boredom are wearing us down. We can end this and get back to normal."

"Can we? Isolation has kept us alive. People who stayed in the cities got eaten. Or went crazy and became eaters."

We'd had this discussion before. It had been civil at first. Jayden's argument was that the plague had run its course. His hypothesis was that the cannibals had run out of food and were dying off.

I urged the committee to be patient. "If they're becoming extinct, all we have to do is wait to be sure. Better than messing up and giving them a meal to sustain them. As far as we know, we're the last humans left. It's our duty as survivors to avoid getting infected. Starve the beasts and we'll hurry their extinction. We'll stay safe and eliminate the threat without sacrificing people."

The committee listened to my advice then. For a while, all was calm. Then I caught a few impatient whispers that repeated Jayden's claim: "Can't win a war without fighting."

Some die-hard survivalists in our group wanted to launch raiding parties. The more recklessly the new arrival from Reno spoke, the more of our group looked to him around the nightly campfire.

"Let's go downtown and play Shoot a Predator before all the targets are gone," Jayden told the committee one night. "It might be our last chance for some target practice."

"Until you're trapped by a horde and run out of ammunition," I said. "You've got this fantasy you can wade in there like it's a video game on easy mode. What happens when you get bitten? Do you expect me to shoot you in the head so you don't turn? How am I going to make time to save you from that ugly fate while we're being overrun? That's a helluva burden you'd be putting on us just so you can experience some wild escapist fantasy. That's not a survivalist fantasy, by the way. It's escapism. I want to escape as much as you do, but the apocalypse shouldn't be an excuse for you to go out and enjoy a few pleasant afternoons shooting people who are out of their minds with hunger and disease."

"But it is, though!" Jayden said. "By your own words, we'd be putting sick people out of their misery. You wouldn't let a starving dog suffer."

"I'm worried you'll feed the starving dog and give him the strength to attack us," I said.

"I'm not the bad guy in this scenario, Nate."

"Then stop getting sexually excited when you clean your rifle, Jayden."

Jayden laughed, good-natured to a fault. He pretended he was joking when he called me Do-nothing Nate. We all had a good laugh, but Jayden and I became enemies the moment he arrived. When he met Cheryl, their eye contact and handshake went on a little too long. I knew he was going to be trouble. I shouldn't have even gotten into the car with him.

At my urging, the committee agreed to wait another month before sending a scouting party deeper into the city. Tension in the camp climbed with the midday heat. People were too idle. There was no farming out in the desert. We lived off canned goods we'd raided from the suburbs. Even playing a card game to pass the time reminded us of the city we'd abandoned for the safety of isolation. The towers of Vegas sat on the horizon, mocking us.

I told everyone, "What happens in Vegas, stays in Vegas. In this case, that means all the killing and disease stays within city limits. You are meat-based and uncooked! Do not feed the zombies!"

Opinion's tide turned in Jayden's favor when he came back from Reno with a five-ton truck full of heavy ordnance. "The National Guard made a stand there. They got overrun, but fortunately for us, the horde moved on. That fight was back when there were so many more hungries. Imagine the mop-up we can do with heavy machine guns now!"

I managed to shoot down Jayden's original plan to take Las Vegas back. He wanted all of us to drive around the city streets firing at every cannibal we saw.

"And what happens when your big truck meets an unforeseen obstacle? For all we know, an overpass or a building has collapsed in the last year."

"Now you're reaching for excuses not to deal with the threat head on," he said. Several of our group nodded in agreement.

"When we went into quarantine," I said, "so much traffic snarled, people abandoned their cars in the middle of the street. You want to go in with no plan and no clear path? What happens when you're surrounded? You're going to get us killed that way."

"But we've got all this firepower and shiny unused ammo now!" he enthused. "We could clean out the hungries in a week!"

"That big truck makes plenty of noise. You'll draw them all out and they'll surround you. You'll be dead within an hour if you blunder in blind. Go if you want, but don't take anyone with you. Worse, maybe you'll just get a few bites taken out of you. If you do make that run to the strip and fail, please don't lead the infected back to camp."

If I hadn't uttered that last sentence, I wouldn't have been in

Jayden's Prius zipping into Las Vegas. I'd meant to push the point home that Jayden was a careless fool, not a hero. However, I'd given him an idea the committee decided was a fine compromise. We wouldn't go into the cannibal's lair. We'd draw them out into the open and shoot them at the city's limits.

"We'll set up a kill zone," Jayden said. "It'll be glorious. Even better, there'll be fewer dead people in the city. The cleanup is going to be a big enough job as is. The more we can lure out of the city, the fewer stinking bodies we'll have to haul ourselves. Nobody wants to survive the zombie apocalypse only to die from some other awful disease festering in the city's corpses!"

"What if there are too many of them? You'd be leading them right to us."

Jayden gave me a smirk that several of the council shared. "We're all in RVs, Nate. We're mobile. Any other concerns or are you just here to shoot down every good idea with nothing good of your own to contribute?"

Despite leading sixty-eight people to safety and organizing them long enough to survive 387 days, suddenly I was Do-nothing Nate, a coward. When the committee voted, even Cheryl gave me a helpless shrug and raised her hand in favor of Jayden's plan.

"There's the marker." Jayden suddenly slowed the Prius and pointed to three bright-orange paint cans in a net sitting in the middle of the road. "This is where I walked back from when I did the first mission! Pretty rad, am I right? I'll take you a few more blocks so you can get the attention of baddies in the area. We'll rendezvous at the paint cans, okay? By then, I'll have the tin cans in the trunk tied to the bunker. Whoever you lure out, we'll drive back slowly, just like last time. We'll be the Pied Piper, bringing the enemy to our guns."

"Pied Piper makes it sound neat and easy," I said, "but I'm bait and I feel like I'm wriggling on a hook."

"That's how it's done if you want to catch the big fish, big guy!"

"Big fish get the hook, but they get the bait, too."

"You worry too much."

"I was an accountant. I do the math."

"That's no way to live. We're men of action now ... or at least I am."

"We're the leftovers after the biggest, ugliest feast in human history."

"The first thing I'm going to do when we clear out Vegas is get you some antidepressants," he said. "And if you won't take them, I will. Your always-say-die attitude is really bumming me out."

I stopped him at five blocks from the marker. "That's plenty. Constant stress has helped me lose some weight, but it's not like I've been working that hard on my cardio. It's too hot to jog out in the desert."

"You, Nate, are what my mama and daddy used to call a whiner."

"Yeah? Didn't you tell me they got eaten on the first day of the outbreak because they didn't believe in it?"

Jayden gritted his teeth and said nothing. Instead, he opened his door abruptly and hurried to get three more orange paint cans out of the trunk. Together in a net, the cans were quite heavy and made a loud clunk when he tossed them on the pavement.

"Sh!" I said. "Be careful! We don't want them popping out at us before we're ready!"

"I'd be fine with that. Whose side are you on, Nate?" He handed me one of the two M-16s he'd scavenged from the National Guard post. Besides the weapons and ammunition, the trunk was full of empty tin cans tied together with string and filled with gravel. After I'd done my duty as zombie bait, the cans would make plenty of noise when dragged behind the vehicle. Our group was waiting to spring the trap on whatever hungries we managed to trawl.

Jayden looked me in the eye and appeared very sincere when he wished me luck. "What we do, we do for the greater good and the survival of our species."

"Good benediction," I said. "You rushed the delivery a little, but fine words."

"You're a ballbuster, man! See you in five blocks. I'll be waiting by the marker. I'll have my noisemakers attached by then. Fire a few shots in the air to get them started and see who answers your mating call, huh?"

"Sure."

Jayden gave me an exaggerated wink. "If you lose confidence, just remember to breathe and run faster. If you mess up, don't worry about Cheryl. I'll give her my best!"

In the few steps it took Jayden to walk from the back of the car to the driver's seat, I pondered shooting him in the back. That wouldn't have made me a hero in anyone's eyes, but I wouldn't have considered myself a coward, either.

He jumped back behind the wheel. As he zipped away, he honked the car's horn long and hard. Startled, I was almost sure I heard him cackle as he drove off in the direction we'd come.

He thought I was a coward and maybe I was. After his first experiment luring the infected into our field of fire succeeded, stupid pride pushed me to take point on the second attempt.

Looking around, there wasn't much to see. The suburban lawns, previously watered diligently by sprinklers and cared for by landscaping companies, were now dry and dead. If we didn't reclaim the city, the desert would eventually take back the land. The houses looked pretty much the same, though from where I stood I spotted two doors hanging open on their hinges. Looters don't close doors behind them. It could be that it was the original owners who left in a hurry, as if there was any place to go. There were rumors of massive refugee camps, but outbreaks hit hard there, too. Some loners, people like me, evacuated successfully and remained healthy because we stayed away from crowds.

My father used to take me hunting back home in Maine. On my first hunting trip with him, we walked through an orchard out in the back of the beyond of Poeticule Bay. "Whether you're hunting game with a camera or a rifle, there's something you need to know. When you go into the woods, stop, stand still, and keep your big mouth shut. When we walked in looking for pheasants, you barreled in like you were tramping into our living room. This is a wild place. Nature is listening."

Before I could speak, he put a finger to his lips and cupped a hand over his left ear.

After an impatient minute, I told him, "The woods are quiet."

"That's because they're still listening for you," he whispered.

What was true in Maine thirty years before was true in the suburbs of Vegas. The last time I'd been this deep in the city, distant sirens were constantly wailing: cops, ambulances, and finally the eerie rise and fall of civil defense sirens. The street was deathly quiet now. Even the breeze died as I stood like a statue.

In the woods, when the forest has accepted your presence, the birds begin to natter at each other again. Small animals, like chipmunks, race through the bush, heedless of human presence. It was the same that day in Las Vegas. Quiet at first ... then the hint of noise in the distance I could not identify. It might have been a door banging open, but there was no wind to make that happen naturally. Closer, maybe in the yards behind the houses to my left, a woman screamed. I'd heard that kind of scream before. When a cannibal killer is excited and makes that sound, a feeding is imminent.

I scanned the sky for birds. Carrion birds often served as a sign of a nearby kill. Finding no scavengers circling overhead, I suspected I was the intended feast. Another cry went up a little farther away.

They're like wolves, I thought. *Jayden and his damn car horn. Is he trying to get me killed? Possibly. Maybe ... probably.*

Assuring myself that I was only spooked because I didn't like Jayden, I dismissed that nagging suspicion. It wasn't easy to stay calm. For a change, I was alone. At the beginning of the pandemic, I'd stayed away from everyone and anyone. After the world's population contracted, I couldn't risk complete solitude anymore. When you're alone, there's no one guarding you while you sleep. And what if I twisted an ankle or strained a back muscle on a supply run? I wasn't old, but at thirty-nine, I wasn't young anymore, either. In a crisis, people need each other. In a zombie apocalypse, having someone around to watch your blind spot is a critical need. Standing alone and out in the open, the loneliness of survival struck me all at once.

Committed to traveling light, I only carried the rifle and a canteen full of water. Jayden had thoughtfully slipped two mags into the pockets of my tactical vest at the small of my back.

"You won't need these," he assured me. "Just for comfort."

I'd worn my steel-toed work boots. In the unlikely event I'd have to defend myself, they'd be good for kicking.

It's only five blocks, I thought. *Keep your head, follow the plan.*

Cupping a palm to my ear, I strained to listen for threats, turning and pausing at each point of the compass. It was quiet, but I didn't believe my ears. I trusted the pressure of apprehension that told me I was being watched. The cannibal killers would not stalk me. They were known for the frenzy of their attacks, not strategy. One or two, if clumsy, weren't typically much of a mortal threat if dealt with correctly. However, just like humans in large groups acting together and driven by awful motivations, they could be deadly.

Screw it, I thought. *Let's get this over with.*

I fired two shots in the air to get their attention, paused, and fired one more to help the infected zero in. I didn't have to wait long. More excited howls went up, closer to my position. More worrying, one of them was *behind* me.

That's the moment I realized the fatal flaw in Jayden's plan to clear the zombies out of Vegas. When they hunted, they tended to form packs or even hordes. We didn't know much. The cannibals were surely drawn by sound (often the terrified screams of their victims). Perhaps scent played a part in their tracking, as well. But when they weren't hunting, they seemed aimless. Some stood still for hours at a time. Others wandered. No one had seen one lie down unless they were wounded or shot in the head.

Jayden's scheme worked on the base assumption that they were still human enough to be drawn to a home base. He had lured twenty-seven zombies to our guns, and we had the bullet-riddled bodies to prove it. As I mourned and prayed over those victims of the plague, he celebrated. Dancing around the fresh corpses, he was drunk on victory. The barrels of our 50 Cals were still hot and smoking as he performed his touchdown dance. Killing was a game to Jayden. We'd seen so much death, I'd hoped the time for illusions and delusions had passed. I was embarrassed for him, but most of the camp cheered him on.

"We're going to take the city back!" Cheryl cried. "If this works, the first thing I'll do is go to the stores and pick out the best food I can find. If that's all spoiled by then, fine. Gotta be some great liquor left over. I'm sick of warm beer."

Still dancing around the fire, Jayden shouted, "I'm gonna take over the Bellagio! Because the house always wins, your first two drinks are on me. I like poker and blackjack. If you're in the mood to lose your rations faster, play roulette! How about you, Nate? You a betting man?"

I was almost sure he'd asked if I was a *better* man.

"We better pile up these bodies before it gets dark. I'll get the kerosene," I told him.

"Bring back the marshmallows and weenies! How about you, Cheryl? You want to make s'mores? Or maybe you're in the mood for a wiener?"

She giggled. My jaw clenched so hard my teeth hurt.

Listening to the howls of the infected, I ground my teeth again. It took discipline to stand still. I almost took off at a sprint to hide in the nearest house with an open door. However, as bait, I had to let them find me before I could start back.

I'd always been a cautious person. An insurance agent once asked me if I parachuted. I laughed in his face. I cooked fish too long so I wouldn't get parasites. Before taking a car out, I circled the vehicle to make sure the tires were properly inflated. I'd been called paranoid and a Nervous Nelly before the world changed. The same character trait that had made me look weak and anxious kept me alive when hordes of the infected roamed the streets.

Caution pulled at me, urging me to start back immediately. However, another niggling worry made my brain itch. If I failed to lure a significant number of the infected into our trap, Jayden would crow about how many more he'd trawled. Worse, my insignificant haul might lead the group to believe that the city was almost empty of pestilence. If that happened, they'd vote to return to the city prematurely.

Every fiber of my being told me returning to Vegas was the nexus of bravery and stupidity. Cars clogged the streets. The city offered more hiding places for humans, but that meant more hidey-holes for the cannibals, too. Living in the desert without air conditioning was often boring and unpleasant, but at least we could always spot the zombies coming.

As I watched the street, two of the infected emerged from a house with an open door. Judging by what was left of their clothes, they'd been young women once. Haggard, with greasy hair hanging in their faces, they growled as they limped forward. The disease had robbed them of their higher faculties so all they managed were low growls that sounded like they had swallowed gravel.

One rare viral variant had allowed the infected to vocalize somewhat. Those monsters called out to their intended victims for help in convincing tones of distress. Then they'd attack, lunging with their teeth, clawing with their nails, and pulling people to the ground to feed. Hyenas, we called those predators. It was the stuff of nightmares, and those encounters still haunted me.

When I lived in Vegas, a couple of hyenas pounded on my door several times in the middle of the night, begging to be let in. I barricaded the door and cowered behind it as I listened to their pleas. Clutching a crowbar to my chest, I sat against the wall and whispered a chant, "They aren't still human. It's a trick. It's a trick. It's a trick."

I might have been lying to myself. Those midnight callers might have been other survivors searching for safety. To assure myself I was still a human being, I had to affirm they weren't. Otherwise, I was worse than the infected. Choosing to turn other survivors away would make me a monster. "I'm a good person. I'm a good person. I'm still a good person," I told myself.

A niggling fear added its voice to my racing thoughts: *But if you have to keep telling yourself that, you probably aren't.*

There was no mistaking the infected now. They could not raise their heads, so it looked like they were staring at the ground. Bent at the waist, the two women coming at me did not limp. They lurched in a shambling gait, each dragging their right leg. I'd seen this before. Someone, a loved one or a sadist, had hobbled them in an effort to make them less dangerous.

It was a strategy some reality-deniers used early on in the pandemic. Such half-measures did not save the infected, nor did the strategy save the uninfected in the end. Keep a zombie around long enough, eventually, you'll lower your guard. Their injuries could impair them, but they were always looking for a chance to strike. At the very least, their well-intentioned keepers were bitten. Just as bravery and stupidity often cross paths, cruelty and kindness can be sisters. That's what I decided to name the two infected struggling to get at me: Cruelty and Kindness.

They were still a couple of hundred feet away. They'd be an embarrassing catch. I needed more fish in my net, so I waited. My hand shook as I took a quick swallow of warm water from my canteen.

When this is all over, I thought, *I'm going to get a bunch of solar panels and hook them up to a freezer and waste all that power just to make ice.*

Cruelty and Kindness were a hundred feet away. The nearest one didn't seem to see me. She stopped abruptly and sniffed the air. A hot bead of sweat slid from my temple and down my cheek as I stared into the face of utter corruption. Smears of blood the color of rust and crimson stained their ruined faces.

Crimson blood! They've fed recently!

My suspicions that Vegas' infestation was far from over were confirmed.

As they drew closer, lines of drool hung from their gaping maws. Their torn clothing revealed emaciated bodies, little more than jutting bones and sinew. Their deterioration made them less dangerous, but their look of hungry determination fed my fear.

Focused on Cruelty and Kindness, I almost missed the attacker coming at me from my right. His footfalls were heavy, but his legs were working fine. With barely enough time to register what was coming at me, I swung the rifle up from my hip and squeezed off two quick shots that caught the zombie in the lower abdomen and the chest. He went down screaming.

My attacker was tall and bald. A bicycle helmet hung behind his head, and the strap under his chin had rubbed his throat raw. Judging by his gear, he'd been a serious cyclist. After the revolution and secession, many had taken up cycling when gas became too expensive and the supply chains failed. I remembered some comedian on television making a moronic quip about how the zombie apocalypse would finally get people to exercise. It's all fun and games until you see someone get eaten.

The cyclist's left arm was bare and hung uselessly, floppy like a rag doll. Several ragged chunks had been bitten out of his forearm, and the flesh around the wounds was black, oozing pus. My stomach turned.

Cruelty and Kindness were so close, I could smell them. As I backed away, the infected women paid no attention to the zombie writhing on the ground. Others disagreed, but I suspected theirs was a lonely existence. It was true they often appeared in groups, but when they were out for blood, they focused only on prey. To one zombie, any other of their kind was just furniture.

Jayden often romanticized their plight, framing them as hunters and seekers. I tried to think of them as patients suffering from the Rage Plague, AKA the Ragin' Contagion. Mad dogs received mercy. Former humans deserved no less. The cyclist struggled to rise. I put one slug in the cyclist's head before turning back.

Another attacker was not forty feet away and closing fast. This one was a young man of maybe seventeen. Judging by his speed and how unsoiled his clothes were, he was a recent recruit to the zombie species. I would have lured him back to the trap to show the others. Unfortunately, he stood between me and escape in Jayden's Prius. Fearing for my life, I shot him in the face.

Thankfully, he went down hard and lay still. I hated it when they were wounded and conscious. When they screamed, I was never sure

if it was pain. Their cries sounded more like anger and frustration. I
wished they didn't sound human at all.

That was my secret reason for disdaining Jayden's trap. I would
rather they die of natural causes, out of my sight. Slow starvation was
cruel, but what I didn't witness couldn't haunt my nightmares.

My comrades called our survivalist camp their prison. I didn't
mind exile so much. For me, the desert was a place of peace and
calm. I was in no rush to return to the city. Our camp at the city's edge
served up only three threats on a daily basis: five venomous species of
snakes, scorpions, and Jayden.

With Cruelty and Kindness still after me, I set off for my
rendezvous with Jayden. *Five blocks,* I thought. *It's just five blocks.*

I had anticipated firing more shots in the air to attract attention.
So far, this experiment was not going as expected. Glancing over my
shoulder, four more of the infected had joined the chase. None of
them were as quick as the fresh one I'd just shot, but it was still a race.
They were the greyhounds. I was the rabbit. Heavy machine gun
crews waited for us at the finish line.

To stay off the menu, I had to stay ahead of them, but I also had to
stay close enough to encourage them to follow me. The pace was
equivalent to a fast walk with occasional breaks into a quick trot.

For the first block, my pursuers could not close the distance. I felt
so confident I was beyond danger that I turned to walk backward. "I
want you guys to know this isn't personal! I'm doing this for the living.
Isn't that what we were always told? Life is for the living? At least, that
was so until y'all came along!"

At the end of the first block, three more cannibals had joined the
pack. Clearly, Jayden's plan was all wrong. The zombie's population
density wasn't predictable enough for this job to be accomplished
safely. However, I had ammunition, a working weapon, and only four
blocks to go. All they had were nails and teeth, an unquenchable
thirst for blood, and the single-minded determination of the
brainless.

My confidence was shaken when I missed my next few shots. I'd
had plenty of practice with a rifle in the past, but standing still and

firing at a target on a range is radically different from popping shots on the run. With cannibals at my back, I didn't dare stop to take more careful aim. Three hungry killers rushed to the front. I slowed, took a breath, and raised the rifle to squeeze off a few rounds before breaking into a run again. I didn't have time to end them with head-shots as I did the cyclist. I aimed for the center mass, fired, and prayed that if they didn't stay down, at least I'd slowed their pursuit.

One of the trio, a short blond man with long hair, fell and could not get up. I must have nicked the spine. The other two made an unearthly racket.

A long time ago in Maine, a neighbor's cat crawled up into his car engine. When the neighbor turned the ignition, a horrible screech came from under the hood. The cat survived, but her tail was shorter. The zombies I shot made a similar noise, but multiplied by two. I winced at the memory of that poor cat, but this was worse. The men on the ground might have been anything once. A doctor. An HVAC technician. A naturopath. Then they became mindless carnivores. Writhing under the hot sun, if they couldn't get up, they'd cook slowly on the pavement where they lay.

Cruelty and Kindness had fallen far behind, but the pursuers' numbers had grown to nine while I was distracted with paring their numbers down. I could not give the zombies I'd shot a wide berth, or I'd cede ground to the killers at my back. I was close enough that the blond I'd thought dead suddenly reached out and grabbed my pant leg. I let out a shriek, and before I could recoil, his other hand closed on my ankle. I kicked his wrist and his grip loosened. Then I stomped his arm at the elbow. I heard a bone snap, but my attacker didn't let go until I ground my heel in hard.

Something brushed the hair at the back of my head, and I shrieked again as I broke into a sprint.

Nine will do, I thought. *I don't have to outdo Jayden now. I just have to survive to tell the tale.*

Once they learned there were still freshly infected zombies in Las Vegas, surely even the most impatient of my group would reconsider their plans to take the city back. All we needed to do was wait. The

Ragin' Contagion would end while we stayed out in the desert drinking hard and counting our blessings. Of course, the pandemic experience had taught me that people had a hard time surviving even when we played the survival game on easy mode. The thoughtless urge to "return to normal" made otherwise reasonable people engage in wishful thinking.

By the end of the third block, I began looking for Jayden's little yellow Prius. I liked him no better, but I was eager to get back into his car.

The burst of adrenaline I got from nearly getting eaten boosted the bounce in my sprint. Near panic, my breathing grew shallow. The problem wasn't my lung capacity or lack of conditioning. Panic came from hyperventilating. I had to power through the ordeal. My hands began to shake. Not so good for aiming a rifle accurately.

By the time I hit the second block, four more zombies were at my heels. The orange paint cans sat in the middle of the street, just where Jayden had left them. His Prius was nowhere in sight.

My first impulse was denial. Jayden was the kind of guy who stops to give you a ride, but then locks the door or keeps rolling forward as you reach for the door handle. However, this was no mere prank. Illusions and delusions were comforting, but I couldn't afford them. Jayden had abandoned me, and that was attempted murder.

Kicking up my pace to a jog, I strove to put some distance between me and my pursuers. The extra effort would burn off some of the adrenaline raging through my bloodstream.

But their footfalls were still too close. Abandoning the plan to lure them to our heavy weapons, I had to eliminate the threat immediately. I broke into a run until I got to the marker. Ejecting the mag, I reached for a fresh one at the small of my back and slapped it home. I raised the weapon and fired at the nearest cannibal.

No effect.

Taking careful aim, I tried again.

No effect.

Blanks! The bastard gave me blanks.

I switched to the last remaining mag with the same result. My rifle was nothing more than a club. The first magazine had a few rounds left, but there was no time to scoop it up from where I'd dropped it on the ground. The fastest hunter came at me with a low growl.

As zombies go, the man looked quite well. Guessing by the yellow stripes above his pant cuffs, he might have been a firefighter. His shirt had been ripped away, and his torso was covered in multiple bites. The trick to smashing anyone hard with a rifle butt is to step into it and throw the hip. It takes some coordination and core strength, but I'd played baseball. Batting practice in Little League was, in theory, great preparation for clubbing zombies to death.

"Everybody needs to do more situps," Mr. Skylar, my little league coach, had taught us. "You can't fire a cannon from a canoe! More situps and pushups will put some giddyup in your get up and go!"

But stepping toward an attacker as they come at you growling is scary. I chickened out at the last second, sidestepped him, and delivered a glancing blow to the back of his head as he passed.

I lucked out with my second attacker. The middle-aged woman came at me with a surprising burst of speed. As I raised the rifle butt instinctively, I caught her in the throat, clotheslining her. She went down hard.

My third attacker was a burlier fellow. As I raised the rifle to block his lunge, he grabbed the gun and wrenched it from my grasp. As the weapon spun away in slow motion, the firefighter knocked me off my feet, and I was slammed to the pavement.

Mr. Skylar was in my head again and he was screaming, "Get up! Get up! Put some giddyup in your get up and go!"

The firefighter scrambled on top of me. I used his momentum and rolled with him, one hand on his throat to keep his teeth away from my neck, the other on his chest. I'd never touched a nearly naked zombie before. Revulsion seemed to give me an added shot of strength and clarity. The ejected mag was within reach. Desperate to escape him before the others piled on and began feasting, I grabbed it and raked the metal across his eyes. I was unprepared for the hot spray of blood. The rifle magazine was slick with it and slipped from my fingers.

In a panic, I brought all the force I could muster in clapping my palms over his ears. The ploy must have burst his eardrums. In a daze, he loosened his grip enough for me to get to my feet.

The burly fellow crowded in and lunged with his teeth, going for my exposed neck. I leaned back just enough that his mouth closed on my vest instead. Like a junkyard dog with a doll, he did not let go. He clamped down and shook his head. I rose up on my toes and bent my knees as I drove an elbow into his collarbone. I heard it snap as his jaws released me and he staggered back.

I wanted to throw up. Instead, I swallowed my gorge as two more killers came at me. These were not new recruits to the Ragin' Contagion army. They emanated the stink of rot. Stick-thin, bald, and flailing, the pair still wore the filthy remnants of hospital gowns. The infection and starvation had ravaged their bodies so thoroughly, I wasn't sure whether they'd been male or female. I had little trouble ducking and weaving and managed to trip them both. Their faces made wet smacks as they hit the pavement.

Sorry, I thought. *I know this is not your fault.*

I leaped and brought all my weight down on the neck of one of the fetid duo and kicked the other in the throat.

There had been nine at my back. The pair of emaciated zombies weren't getting back up. Cruelty and Kindness were still shambling in the distance. Blinded and deafened, the firefighter appeared confused, wandering off and clutching at the air.

The rifle sat nearby on a yellowed lawn, but the paint cans were closer. A heavy weight does not require ammunition or reloading. I grabbed the net of paint cans and began swinging. I would like to say it was as easy as striking each of my attackers in the head once. In movies, people get knocked out so easily. In real life, much more force and determination are required. It wasn't enough to hit each one once or even five times.

Once they went down, I had to grab the net with both hands and swing the paint cans like an ax and bring all my force down on their heads. The skull is a vault of bone. Using the net full of heavy paint cans as a weapon was a contest between physics and biology.

When I was done, seven cannibal killers lay in the street. I stood over them, sweating and panting. I felt relief but there was no joy in this victory. If we'd just left them alone, and let nature take its course, I would have still been resting comfortably in our desert encampment, safe and guiltless.

Surveying my grisly work, I wished I still had a working cell phone. Not only could I have called for rescue, but I would also have pictures of the burly man. If a zombie could remain that fat and muscular, he'd clearly been feeding on new victims recently and regularly. The crisis in Las Vegas was nowhere near over.

Cruelty and Kindness were almost upon me as I gathered up the rifle and mags. "I've had enough for today, ladies. I'm exhausted but I think I can still outrun you."

I left the street and trotted over to the nearest house. The door was closed and locked, but the front door had glass in it. I used the rifle butt to smash the glass. Reaching through, I found the deadbolt and threw the lock. Cruelty and Kindness struggled up the driveway as I entered the house.

The house had been a nice split-level with a large, well-appointed kitchen with marble countertops and an industrial-level espresso machine. Assuming the human race eventually bounced back from global tragedy, no one would be constructing such luxuries again for another 300 years.

I made a beeline for the back door and closed it behind me. Cruelty and Kindness might find their way out, but I was already cutting through backyards and headed for a parallel street. They posed no threat to me, and I was so sick of Jayden's experiment, I didn't have it in me to put them out of their misery.

Before the pandemic, very few people thought about animals freezing to death or dying of old age in the wild. When I was little, my father brought home a doe he'd shot. He hung the carcass from a tree in the backyard and dressed it. I can close my eyes and still remember the feeling of its velvety fur beneath my fingertips. But it was the doe's big soft brown eyes that captured me. As my father cut off its head, I wept for her.

"This is what the good Lord put these creatures on Earth for, Nathaniel," Dad told me. "Better for me to kill it with one quick shot than for it to starve or freeze to death in the winter when it gets old. Cold and old is a deadly combination."

I should have put Cruelty and Kindness down. I was too tired and had to get back to camp. Let their erasure come by someone else's hand or let God or the Devil do it.

It was a long walk. I doubled back several times, but Jayden must have been confident I would perish. I scanned the street, wary for a bullet from the bushes. The bright yellow Prius was not to be found. He'd returned to camp, sure I could not survive on my own.

Traveling stealthily takes much more time than going for a pleasant stroll. I'd been grateful for my heavy work boots during the fighting, but I soon wished I'd brought along running shoes, too.

I would spend that night in a house at the city's edge. Before I chose a house in which to hide, I'd foolishly drank the last of my canteen. There was no food or water. I retreated to an upstairs bedroom, dozing occasionally, but mostly sleepless, waiting and wary, eager for dawn. I didn't remember raiding this particular residence, but given its proximity to the city's edge, it was probably people from our group of survivalists who'd ransacked this place.

I thought about heading out in the dark. The moon was full, so the way would have been navigable. However, I heard something outside and went to the bedroom window to peer through the blinds. I couldn't make anything out at first. It went so quiet for a couple of moments that I wondered if my nerves were playing tricks on me. Then it came again, a far-off banging. I guessed that someone was striking metal with wood, maybe a wooden picket fence stake against a car's hood.

Cheryl once speculated the zombies were getting smarter if they picked something up and used it as a weapon. I shot that hypothesis down because I'd worked in a zoo one summer and saw a bear dancing. One of my coworkers recorded a video and set music to the bear's frenzied movements. The chief zookeeper made my friend pull the video from her social media. It wasn't dancing. The bear was making frenzied movements because it was agitated and in captivity.

"There's a reason they call RABID-24 the Ragin' Contagion," I told Cheryl. "They're frustrated animals with a virus that's taken over their brains and made them violent. If they bang on something, they aren't drumming. They're angry because they aren't eating."

Looking back, I wondered if that was the beginning of Cheryl's subtle eddies of discontentment with me. We were strangers who met at the camp. Emotions ran high. She thought I was a good partner to have by her side in the apocalypse. She was strong and had plenty of experience in violent situations. She informed me we were a good match. I asked her to move into my RV. I'll say this much for the end of the world: Marriage takes a lot less planning and paperwork.

But maybe I talked through my thoughts too much. Prone to anxiety and depression, my prescription meds had run out, so I relied on Cheryl's support more and more. Meanwhile, Jayden was always sunny and optimistic and rarely had a cogent thought in his head that could contradict any of Cheryl's opinions.

The far-off banging stopped, but I heard footfalls outside. Low moans reached me. The infected were ranging through the neighborhood. Several possible scenarios disturbed me. Had Jayden's scheme attracted enough of the cannibal killers to form a horde that would wander out into the desert and overrun our encampment? Maybe they'd followed me by scent or simply taken the direction of my escape as a compass point that would lead them to me, or worse, back to camp. Would I return only to find Cheryl partially eaten and coming for my throat? I couldn't bear to lose her. Even if I survived, should the camp scatter, I could end up alone again.

Three silhouettes stepped into the street directly in front of my hiding spot. Pale moonlight shone on their upturned faces. The infected stood, staring up at the moon, swaying like reeds in a light breeze.

"What goes on in your heads?" I whispered. "What do monsters think about? Nothing ... I hope."

Something moved in the front yard, and I cursed myself for speaking aloud. Surely, they couldn't have heard me, but they *were* close. I squeezed my eyes tight and held my breath.

How did you bastards find me? Is it going to be me staring up and worshipping the moon next? Or will they all converge so I simply die? And which fate suits me better?

Their moans reached for me like fetid, grasping fingers. Unable to withstand the suspense any longer, I decided to look into the face of doom and peered out again.

The street, the lawn, everywhere. Dozens of the infected lurched toward me. A horde is a terrible thing to witness. There are no individuals in it. A horde is a force of nature, as mindless and undefeatable as a tidal wave. Even with our 50 cals, we would have a hard time mowing them all down before they reached us. The power of mindlessness is that zombies do not run from gunfire. Where humans would run, retreat, or take cover, the infected were heedless to anything but hunger. They just kept coming.

One of them hit the front of the house. I could almost picture Jayden's smirking face. "Somebody's knocking at the door, Nate. Don't be rude. Go let them in. End this. You can be mindless, too. And wouldn't that be freeing? Join the dummies and never have a moment's doubt or even a niggle of fear enter your noggin again! Your deletion from the human race really is the perfect solution for all of us, especially Cheryl and me."

More pounding sounded at the front door.

As quietly as possible, I tiptoed to the rear of the house to see if my escape route was clear. *I'm going to have to run for it. But it's seven miles back to camp. I can't run seven miles, and I can't lead them back to camp! Correction,* I thought. *I could lead them back to kill Jayden. I just shouldn't.*

I made my way down the hall to the baby's room. I was thankful the house was free of corpses. Many abandoned homes looked clear from the outside, but suicides were not uncommon. When order was lost and society broke down, the disease drained hope away. Quite a few people decided to end their misery on their own terms. Still, abandoned rooms led me to ask questions. I didn't like the possible answers. What happened to all those poor souls? No one knew how many survivors remained. There was no sanctuary to escape to where worries were erased, and everything had gotten back to normal. That left the many dead, the rabid murder machines, and me.

With trembling fingers, I pulled back a curtain. What I saw there made me need to urinate immediately. I stepped away to pee in the baby's crib. That done, I took a few deep breaths and returned to the window. Before daring to peek out again, I told myself I could not have seen what I thought I did.

A trick of the light, I thought. *A fear-induced hallucination, perhaps. Or a nightmare.*

This was a nightmare, but I was indeed awake. I went from window to window, to the front of the house, and back to the nursery. It took me a few moments to process what I was experiencing. This was no longer a house. I was trapped in a ship on a silent sea of the infected. As the moon slipped from cloud cover, the truth was revealed. They swayed, lurched, and shambled. A few even crawled. Try as I might, I could not see the edges of the tide. The swath and the swarm had no beginning nor end. The killers were far more resilient, persistent, and numerous than Jayden's speculations.

Is it the moon? I wondered. *Is it the lamp, and are you the moths?*

I might have been the first living person to stand amid such a throng. It was perhaps the first time I understood the enormity of the pandemic. Big numbers are difficult to visualize. The threat was always deadly serious, of course, but I'd always thought of it on a personal level. The zombies were coming to kill *me*. As pessimistic as I was, I always thought humans would somehow survive the onslaught. I'd never truly thought of RABID-24 as an extinction-level event. *Attempted* genocide, surely, but until I saw how many mindless killers were out there at once, I had not understood the math. Humans could be gone just as completely from disease as dinosaurs had been wiped out by a giant meteor.

I watched and worried for an hour before I realized there was nothing to do. As the sun rose, I began to worry I might be spotted at my lonely observation post. If they came in, I would die. Paradoxically, that realization was liberating. It would either happen or it would not. I went back to the front bedroom, lay down, and went to sleep.

Waking at noon, I got up, stiff and slow. The yellowed lawn was trampled, but other than that, there was no sign of the tide that had washed over the neighborhood through the night. Perhaps hunger had driven the monsters to migrate. Or maybe some change in the disease process had transformed the zombies into a nocturnal species, repulsed by the Nevada sun, emerging from their lairs at night to roam in some unholy rite known only to their fevered brains. For all I knew, my fanciful notions were true: Maybe the homicidal congregation had united to worship the moonlight.

Shaken, hungry, and thirsty, I emerged from my hiding place, and with the sun beating on my head, I set off on the long trek back to camp. Several times, I stopped at empty houses along the way, sometimes for rest and shade, but usually because my body was a bucket of jangling nerves. Sure I would come upon more killers at every corner, I traveled slowly, preserving my energy in case I needed to make a quick sprint back into hiding.

I made a mental note that if we ever did reenter the city, we had to establish safehouses with supplies and arms. That way when a situation went south, we'd have agreed upon waypoints to which we could retreat. I had a lot to tell the camp. But how would we handle Jayden's crime? Exile, I supposed. Everyone had to pull their own weight, and we did not have a jail.

When I get back, I thought, *I'm going to tell everyone what I saw. That will turn the tables and make everyone rediscover patience and gratitude.*

But, in reality, how many would believe me? The group was so tired of living in the desert. Judgment flags when we are fed up. With all of Jayden's happy talk about the worst of the crisis being over, they might be difficult to convince. Even I had wanted to believe Jayden. Worse, I'd been with the group longer, but he'd made more friends.

I could only guess at what he might have told them. If he dared to say he saw me die, then his credibility would evaporate upon my return. Were I him, I would have told everyone that I failed to show up at the rendezvous point. That way, he'd maintain plausible deniability and could welcome me with open arms even though we both knew the truth. If I objected, he'd tell everyone around the campfire that I was Do-nothing Nate, holing up for a day and a night, and lacking the courage to advance their dreams.

The walk home was slow, but as my shadow grew longer, I had plenty of time to make arguments in my head, countering whatever he might say. I'd done the same thing before everything went to hell, anticipating problems that rarely actually occurred. By the time I spotted the cooking fires and the largest RVs of our encampment, I thought I was ready to face Jayden.

But a new thought struck: What if Jayden was on watch? Darkness had begun to fall. If he shot me to death, all he'd have to do was claim I was infected. He could say my death was a cruel kindness.

Parched and desperate for a drink, I made myself wait. The beautiful sunset served as my sole distraction from that aching need. The sun seemed to drop more quickly in the desert than it ever had in Maine.

I lay down and waited for the stars to come out. With no light pollution, the Milky Way looked so close. If the zombies worshipped the moon, I worshipped the stars. In the billions upon billions of galaxies, there must be many planets where peace reigned, death was never violent, and betrayal is unknown.

It was late as I made my way toward our encampment. I approached at an angle and stayed low. Near the edge of camp, I spotted a tall figure and a tiny light. There was no mistaking John Bennett, the oldest man in camp. I suspected he only took guard duty so he could smoke in peace. His wife Mary was a sweet woman who taught knitting, sewing, and cooking to anyone who wanted to learn. I only ever saw her get angry with her husband when she caught John smoking.

I'd once witnessed her in high dudgeon. "You wanna die of lung cancer when there isn't an oncologist left in the whole damn world, old man?"

"Well, hell, yeah, you're making it kind of appealing, old woman," John replied. That was also the only time I'd seen John run.

I was quite close to camp before I tried whistling at him. Zombies do not whistle. However, my mouth was so dry, I couldn't manage it.

"John! It's me!"

Startled, the old man whirled. "Who goes there?"

"Who goes there? What are you? A castle sentry from another century?"

"Well, I am from another century! That you, Nathaniel Bixby?"

"The same."

He slung his rifle back on his shoulder. "How you doin', man?"

"Parched."

"Better than dead. Thought you were dead."

"That what Jayden told you?"

"Said you didn't show up, missed your appointment. He stayed around a long time waiting on you. Didn't get back until after dark last night. He was pretty upset."

"He's a liar. Got anything to drink?"

He handed me an unopened beer from his jacket pocket. I didn't ordinarily care for beer, but I drank it all at once.

"Got any more?"

"No, but you better slow down if you haven't had anything much."

A bout of dizziness swept over me but it soon passed. I told John I had bigger worries. "Las Vegas still belongs to the infected. Masses of them."

"Bad news. Mary will be relieved. I keep telling her that once we head back home, I plan to take up with a showgirl. I told her she could have a pool boy, but she wouldn't budge on the issue unless she got two pool boys. I told her we're too old for that much excitement."

He took a long drag on his cigarette and let the smoke stream out in a long sigh. "And here we are stuck, huh? Jokers and clowns, the dead and the mostly dead. Sometimes I look in the mirror and wonder which of the above is me. I check a lot of boxes, young Nathaniel."

"I saw a horde, John. And Jayden left me to die."

"That so?"

"It is."

"I'd call the cops for you, but they're all indisposed, eating black and brown folks exclusively, I imagine."

"He took off on me, so I guess we'll have to expel him for his crimes."

John was quiet for a moment, then nodded sagely. "That would be the biblical eye for an eye approach. Hell of a thing to do to a person in this world, ain't it? Sending him off in the desert with a canteen and nothing but finger guns to shoot with. Jayden's got a lot of friends in camp. I imagine somebody might give him a ride back to Reno."

As long as he was away from me, I'd be satisfied with that outcome.

"Sleep on it," John advised. "The whole camp can hear your story in the morning."

"It's not a story. It happened."

"Not what I meant, buddy. I can see you're on your last nerve. Take it easy."

I entered our circle of RVs and tents. Everyone was asleep. Before I headed to my camper, I stopped at the bus which served as our armory. The door was always unlocked for quick access in an emergency. I kept my rifle, but picked up three fresh magazines.

"Full metal jacket, useful, and the way it ought to be," I muttered.

I didn't even know how Jayden got hold of blanks. I guessed he'd had to make them himself.

That's pre-meditation, I thought, *and I still have the dummy mags as proof.*

I was already planning my summation to the jury as I opened the door to my camper. My plan was to drink everything we had, rehydrate, and wake Cheryl to say her boyfriend was not dead.

It was not the tearful reunion I envisioned. Cheryl was awake and she was with her new boyfriend. They were both naked. As soon as I spotted him lying next to her in my bed, I raised the rifle.

Jayden raised his hands. "Dude! Take it easy! It was all her idea!"

Cheryl slapped him across the face as hard as she could. That was pretty hard. I didn't object. I pointed the rifle at her and waited for an explanation. Cheryl gave him another smack in the head, really winding up this time.

"*Ow! Jesus!* You got me in the ear! Don't hit somebody in the ear!"

"Jerk!" she shouted. "You said you took care of him!"

I cleared my throat. "When I said I'd take care of you, I meant I'd try to protect you and always care for you. You meant something else, didn't you?"

She had nothing to say that might exonerate her, but there wasn't really that much to say. Even at gunpoint, Cheryl was too smart to attempt a lame excuse.

"You could have just dumped me," I said.

"But it's *your* RV," Jayden said. "In a divorce, you have to split things up. Times being what they are, she thought you'd just kick her out. Living in a tent beside my little car wasn't good enough for her." He actually had the nerve to sound hurt.

"Shut up, Jay!" Cheryl told him. "You're making it worse."

"I don't think it's going to get much worse," I said. "That's her reasoning. Why'd *you* want me out of the way?"

Jayden couldn't repress his smile. "Love, Nate. I did it for love."

"And my RV."

"He said you're a drag, Nate," Cheryl said. "You're mad, but you know he's not wrong. You're slowing things down because you're afraid all the time. We all want to get back to living in the city. You don't even want to try."

"Enough! This is much less complicated than we're making it. Come with me."

They got out of bed and began to reach for their clothes.

"Leave 'em," I said.

They didn't want to listen to me, but I wasn't Do-nothing Nate, anymore. I was Nate With a Gun, and Nate with a Gun was ramped up, oozing with giddyup.

The pair of them barely fit in the Prius's cargo space. Under different circumstances, I imagined that might have suited them just fine. I grabbed a few bottles of water and instant lemonade from Jayden's tent and climbed behind the wheel.

John spotted me, walked up, and knocked on my window. "What's up?"

"I am."

"What are you doing, son?"

"This is the only way I get to enjoy air conditioning anymore. You could say I need to clear the air."

"Mr. Bennett? Is that you?" Cheryl shouted. "We're in the trunk! Nate's gone crazy!"

The old man bent over and looked me in the eyes. "Mary and I just kid each other about pool boys and showgirls. You know that, right? We would never."

"I know, John."

He bobbed his head. "If anybody asks, you told me you were taking that pair halfway to Reno and dropping them off with friends. That the plan?"

"Sure."

"Safe travels, then. Remember, for every mile of road, there's two miles of ditches."

"You're a wise man," I said.

"You're a little silly," he replied.

"You knew about Jayden and Cheryl, huh?"

"Everybody did. I can't imagine how you missed it."

"There's a virus going around. It's called magical thinking. The only antidote is a harsh dose of reality."

I drove on. The car was fully charged from a day of being hooked up to the solar panel array, and the road outside the city was clear. The ride might have been silent except for all the crying, shouting, and begging from the back. I preferred oldies radio stations that played the hits, but listening to Jayden's pleas for mercy was almost as good. Hearing Cheryl cry brought me no pleasure, but I was crying, too, and for better reasons.

I didn't know for sure where I was going, but my target was big enough I was confident I'd find it. I'd seen the direction the horde had been moving the night before. The challenge was to get ahead of it. I worried they might circle back to the city's center. Fortunately, though they were terrifying, they did not travel fast. I finally found the forward edge of the tide.

The ride was rough. I had to make some sharp turns to avoid stragglers and barreled off the road at several points. Jayden and Cheryl screamed louder and demanded to know what I was doing.

"We're on a roller coaster!" I yelled back. "Hang on!"

They got quiet for a little while after that. I guessed they might be trying to get at the tire iron to take a swing at me when I released them. Maybe it was just stunned silence, though. They were so used to Do-nothing Nate, they never expected Giddyup Nate to make an appearance.

"I used to be a certified public accountant!" I yelled at the zombies I passed. I'd drunk the beer on an empty stomach, but it had only been one. It probably wasn't the alcohol talking. Giddyup Nate had taken the wheel, and tired of all the bullshit the world had fed him, he was a little crazy. As Giddyup Nate gleefully explained to the passing cannibals, "Time for some biblical justice!"

When I was sure I'd gotten ahead of the horde, I slammed on the brakes. I pulled a U-turn so the car's headlights were pointed in the direction of the lead predators. I couldn't see them yet, but I fired a few shots in the air and laid on the horn for good measure to make sure they were still headed our way. Then I opened the hatch and motioned for my prisoners to get out.

Cheryl and Jayden climbed out stiffly, rubbing their heads. "You're a bad driver," Jayden said.

"You left me to die."

"So? We're even steven, right?"

I had to smile. "You are a charming rat, but you're still a rat."

Cheryl tried a different tack. "Take us back to camp. This is why justice is doled out by impartial people, not by the victims. You can't leave us out here, Nate. If you do this, you're no better than us."

"I am quite confident I'm better than you," I replied. "Besides, I'm going to help you fulfill your dream. A huge horde is coming. That's gotta be a big chunk of Vegas's zombie population."

Jayden was slow on the uptake. "Say what now?"

"Lead them away. Take off in that direction. Is that north? I think that's north."

"There's nothing that way for a hundred miles or more, Nate!" Cheryl said.

"That's kind of the idea. Run until you can't run anymore. You were a runner, Cheryl. You might even live. The kicker about zombies is they may not be fast, but they never sit down. They never rest. They just keep coming. If you want to live, never stop running."

"We're so naked, we don't even have shoes!" Jayden yelled.

Cheryl smacked him across the back of the head and hissed in a stage whisper. "Shut your mouth. Do you want to draw them to us?"

"They're already coming," I said. "I made sure of it. And Jayden? You're barefoot, but I had to run for my life in heavy boots — my steel-toed workboots." I kicked him hard in his right shin.

Jayden grabbed his leg, moaned, and cursed.

"If you lose confidence, just remember to breathe and limp faster. I'll be driving ahead of you for a while to make sure you stay on track. Leave the road and I'll shoot you."

"Bastard," Cheryl said.

"Oh, who knows? Maybe you'll think of something to convince me I should let you back in the car. Choose your words carefully, though. This isn't a situation where you want to waste your breath. I know from very recent experience."

Cheryl had been covering her breasts and her crotch with her hands. She reached out with both arms, inviting me to embrace her. "Put down the gun, Nate. This isn't you."

"I am what circumstances made me. No, maybe I'm what *you* made me. Doesn't matter. I doubt I ever knew you at all. Better set off. You could stop to stretch your hamstrings first, but I'd take advantage of the head start if I were you. Take my advice. Yesterday, I was you."

Cheryl was smarter than Jayden. She took off, headed north as instructed. I had to threaten him with getting shot in the foot to get him going. His departure was timely, too. The horde was so close, I had to hurry to get behind the wheel before the fastest of the horde beat me to the car door.

Honking the horn and flashing the headlights, I backed up and went after the lovers who hated me. Passing Jayden as he limped along, we each flipped middle fingers at each other. Giddyup Nate rolled down the window and called out, "I knew we had to have something in common!" I slowed the car a fraction. "Get in!"

"Really?"

"No." I drove off. I kept an eye on him in the rearview mirror. Jayden did not make it five blocks. The horde swallowed him, first figuratively, then literally.

Cheryl had been quite an athlete all her life and sheer terror got the muscle memory to kick in. When she started to ease her pace, I left a bottle of water and lemonade powder for her on the blacktop. If the horde began to lose interest or direction, I doubled back and honked the horn to get them back on task.

I couldn't help looking for Jayden in the mob, but there'd been so many cannibals, it was unlikely he'd merely been bitten. He must have been devoured completely. Perhaps, by morning, some straggler might find a morsel or would have to settle for sucking the marrow from his bones.

Judas hanged himself, I thought. *That fate was quite merciful.*

When dawn touched her, Cheryl walked with a limp and left a trail of blood from both feet. It was only then, in the light of day, that I began to doubt myself. Punishment for attempted murder was warranted, but was torture ever right? I'd loved this woman only yesterday. I'd been so grateful for her presence in my life, I never suspected the truth of our pairing.

I stopped the car and got out. "You've done well," I told her.

"Bastard!"

"You said that before. I can't say you're exactly wrong."

She gritted her teeth and bent over, hands on knees, trying to catch her breath. "You gonna let me in the car now? He's dead so there's no one to be jealous of."

"I'm not jealous. I'm hurt and angry."

"But are you done?"

I might have been finished with it all then and there, but I noticed she never said she was sorry. "It's not like I could ever trust you."

"You couldn't trust me before, but we were happy for a while, weren't we?"

"I was. Then you tried to have me killed."

She shrugged. "Nobody's perfect."

"Maybe that's my problem. I thought you were perfect. I expected you to keep on being perfect. That's not reasonable is it?"

She shook her head and took deep breaths. "I can't do this much longer, Nate. Then you'll have to live with what you've done. It's not going to be worth it. You're mad now, but when you cool off, you'll see you overreacted."

"You were pretty cool and calculating when you overreacted, wouldn't you say?"

"I'm sorry! All right? *I'm sorry!*"

"Finally!"

She looked back over her shoulder. In the light of day, the mass of zombies was even more horrifying than at night. Their front line had transformed into a long phalanx that stretched far beyond the width of the road. In sunlight, they looked less like a horde and more like an invading army.

"They're coming! Let me in the damn car!"

"One more mile."

"Nate!"

"I'll be waiting for you one more mile up the road. Have you got it in you?"

"No!"

"I think you do. One more mile, Cheryl. That's all I ask."

I got back in the car and drove off. She almost touched the rear fender before I accelerated away.

With my eye on the odometer, I hit the brakes at exactly one mile from where I left her. I got out and looked around. There was a shack far off in the distance to my left. To my right, nothing but desert and a defunct wind turbine. Did big wind turbines have a door with a lock in the bottom? Could someone hide and survive in one of those? I had no idea.

After several minutes of debate, I looked in the glove compartment and found the registration papers and a pen. I scribbled a note and left it in the middle of the road under the last bottle of water. I left her a packet of lemonade powder, the rifle, and the mags of ammunition.

As I pulled away, I caught sight of Cheryl in the rearview mirror. The zombie army was gaining on her. It is unlikely that I could have heard her screams. I thought I did, though. Glancing in the rearview, I watched her until she was a dot.

The open road beckoned. I couldn't imagine returning to the Vegas encampment. Instead, I'd keep going until the Prius's charge ran out. Then I'd walk until I was somewhere I'd never been before. Somewhere new where I could be new.

I wasn't sure who the new guy would be. Do-nothing Nate was a sap, and Giddyup Nate could be mean. With time and distance, maybe I could learn something from Jayden. I could take on his sunny attitude and optimism. Armed with that skill, maybe I could even make new friends who knew nothing of the old me.

My note had read: *Maybe you saved Las Vegas. Thanks for that and I'm sorry, you were right. Nobody's perfect. I forgive you. Good luck!*

Cheryl probably didn't have time to read it, though. A single shot rang out as I drove away.

I did not look in the rearview mirror again.

CLARITY

Emma Dunn spotted the man by the side of the road. Since he was lying in the shade of a tree, she took him for dead. The zombies sometimes paused to listen and smell the air, but they never lay down unless they were shot in the head. Emma crouched in the bushes, scanning in all directions, wary of a trap.

The man rolled over to reveal a backpack that lay beside him. Emma was sure he was still human then. Creeping closer, she picked up a rock and threw it at the tree trunk above his head. He startled awake, but did not move quickly. She thought he might be addled in some way, perhaps bitten or sick. After a moment of looking around, he lay back with his head on his backpack and croaked, "If you're going to kill me, whoever you are, I wish you'd get on with it. I'm exhausted."

"Are you bitten?" Emma called out.

"No," the man said. "Haven't even seen a rabid cannibal in days."

"What are you out here for?"

"Traveling."

"You from around here?"

The man shook his head but did not attempt to figure out where Emma was hiding. He hadn't pulled a weapon, either.

If he had one, surely he would have pulled it out by now, Emma reasoned.

"Where's your group?" Emma asked.

"Don't have one. Where's yours?"

"They're around."

"I'm not carrying much so not much point robbing me. If you aren't planning to kill me, I imagine I'll go back to my nap, if that's okay by you?"

The man pulled his hat down over his eyes and did indeed appear to fall back asleep. Intrigued, Emma wondered why anyone would travel alone unless they were suicidal. He didn't ask her for anything. That set him apart from everyone else she'd come across. Everyone always wanted something, whether it be food, water, shelter, company, or mercy.

Emma emerged from her hiding place, her spear at the ready. She crossed the road and stood at a safe distance to assess what threat he might pose. His clothes were ragged and filthy, and his sneakers were very worn. His beard was long and unkempt. He'd obviously been traveling on foot for a long time. "Hey!"

The man got up on one elbow and eyed her spear and the dirty, rusty machete tucked into her cloth belt. For armor, she wore magazines taped to her forearms. Her blonde hair was tied back in a very long ponytail. She was lean, muscular, and sharp-eyed. If not for her jeans and the copies of muscle magazines, she might have been a tall Scandinavian warrior.

"Where you headed?" Emma asked. "If you're thinking of going up to the FEMA camps in Portland, they've been overrun. Border to Canada is closed, which wouldn't mean much, except what's left of *our* military is making sure no one else can go farther north."

The man sat up. "Well, that's uncharitable, but I thought I'd get up to Brookings. Where am I now?"

"Just outside of Klamath Falls."

"Oregon? I made it to Oregon?"

Emma broke into a grin. "You did! What's in Brookings?"

"I heard there's a nice beach there. I grew up by the Atlantic. I thought it might be good to see the Pacific before I die. Always had an obsession with symmetry."

"It's just water. Can't even drink it."

The man shrugged. "I was hoping for a nice view. How far is it from here?"

"If the roads weren't blocked, and if you had any gas, three hours. Things being what they are, three or four days, I'd guess."

The man cursed and flopped back on the ground.

Emma put one hand on her hip and considered the stranger for a moment. He was not only ragged, his arms and legs were stick-thin. He didn't appear to pose much of a threat. "Not many tourists in the apocalypse."

"Not much of anything in the apocalypse. I miss going to movies and dining out in restaurants. What about you?"

Emma ignored the question and poked his sneakers with the butt of her spear. "C'mon. I know a place you can dine. Jesus, when's the last time anyone used the word *dine*? Anyway, you coming, stranger?"

He gave her a toothy grin. "Depends. What's on the menu?"

"Can of beans?"

He nodded and with some effort, got to his feet. "I could use some protein. Been chewing tree bark and grubs."

She gestured for the man to follow, and he did so, limping along slowly at a respectful distance beyond the swing of her spear. "You sure you haven't been bit recently? For some, the turn doesn't happen right away."

"Weird they never figured out why, huh? But, no, I move like an old man because I'm exhausted and my feet hurt. I'm looking forward to those beans, but I'm so tired, I might have to ask you to chew them for me."

Emma chuckled and asked where he was from.

"South. Walked across the state of Idaho."

"*Really?* Why?"

"Because I don't have a pilot's license, and my arms aren't wings. Sure wouldn't want to get in trouble with the FAA."

She chuckled again. "I can't remember the last time I saw a plane in the air."

"Me, neither. Kinda makes me wish I had learned to fly."

"Where would you go?"

"Anywhere with the fewest people. That's what passes for safe these days, I guess."

"By that measure, it's pretty safe around here. What did you see in Idaho?"

"Devastation."

"So ... just Idaho, then."

"That's not nice. Idaho has several good points. Besides the potatoes, there's the fact that it's pretty much emptied out."

"Is that why you don't seem to be carrying a weapon?"

"I'm not strapped, but, no, that's not why."

He said nothing more and Emma didn't push. She'd met several strangers attempting to pass through Klamath Falls. Most of them didn't open up about their trauma right away, and the ones that did spew their tearful history right out of the gate were insufferable. Everyone had suffered so no one was special.

As they walked on in silence, houses appeared on either side of the road.

He cleared his throat and spat. "What were you doing out in the woods, if I may ask?"

"Hunting rabbits, birds, frogs, and whatever."

"And you found nothing?"

"I was on my way out when I found you."

He sighed. "Finding me is close to finding nothing." After a moment, he cleared his throat again. "Sorry, I'm a bit down, and the end of the world plays hell with my self-esteem issues. I'd book an appointment with a therapist, but they're all dead."

Emma pointed to a yellow house coming up on their right. "You're going to see something in a second. Promise me you won't freak out."

"I can't promise much, but I don't think I have the energy for a full-on freakout."

The house was large with an overgrown yard. Crouched in the tall grass, a zombie in an advanced state of decay peered at them and growled. He had no arms.

"He's tied up," Emma said, "so he'll give us no trouble."

"What is that poor fella's story?"

"That's Clay Filmore. He used to own a restaurant in town."

"And?"

"Let's just say that when the outbreak came to Klamath, he did the opposite of helping. Even when there was an outbreak at Sky Lakes Medical Center, he told everybody it was a hoax. Then he said it wasn't that bad. Zombies are slow, so why worry? And while those in charge waffled and debated, the world fell down."

The man grinned. "Who was it who said something about the danger of underestimating the power of dumb people in large groups?"

Emma shrugged. "I'd look it up, but we haven't had internet since it helped to kill us by spreading lies and propaganda."

"Preaching to the choir, miss."

The woke corpse that had once been Clay Filmore lunged at them, but the chain around his neck brought him up short.

"One of these days, if I walk by often enough, that chain will deliver enough friction that he'll decapitate himself. Then my revenge will be complete." Emma smiled.

The man said nothing. Emma couldn't guess whether he was judging her or his silence signified tacit agreement. "What happened to his arms?"

Emma shrugged. "Leprosy, maybe?"

"No, really."

"Thresher accident? Hay balers do that sort of thing, don't they?"

"C'mon, Miss."

"A long while ago, ol' Clay there, with all the respect he was actually due, got the day he deserved."

"How do you even go about chaining up one of them?" he asked.

"You have to get them tied down while they're newly bit. If you don't catch them early, it gets more difficult and dangerous. It becomes a whole animal control thing, loop on a pole and whatnot."

"And what are you? The local dog catcher?"

"Around here? I like to think of myself as the justice of the peace."

Farther on, a scattering of vehicles clogged the street. For a time, early in the pandemic, Klamath Falls had isolated itself, turning travelers back and refusing to allow anyone to leave. When store stocks ran short, the city allowed trucks to deliver supplies again. However, the supply chain itself soon broke, and no more trucks came. When the outbreak at the hospital spread out into the community, no one wanted to go through Klamath Falls anymore, and everyone wanted to leave.

"How many survivors remain?" the man asked.

"Don't know. Not many. The census taker is definitely dead."

Finally, they came to a cul-de-sac ringed by five large houses. The man followed Emma to the biggest house and stepped over the trip wires she pointed out to him. Once they made it safely to the front door, she took a key from around her neck and turned the lock.

It was dark inside, but as Emma turned on an electric lantern, her treasure trove was revealed. Shelves laden with canned goods, batteries, protective gear, and cleaning supplies stood in the front hallway. The man paused to take it all in. "With all this, why go hunting?"

"Fresh meat is better. I'm trying to make the canned goods last."

"Keep an eye on the expiry dates so you don't lose out on a good meal."

Emma gave a long sigh.

"Sorry," he said. "Just trying to help."

"Of the two of us, who looks like they're handling the end of the world better?"

He nodded. "You, obviously. So ... how about those beans?"

Emma tossed her head, inviting him deeper into the house, but she did not put her spear aside. She led him to a large kitchen. Light streamed through the floor-to-ceiling windows. A vegetable garden took over most of the fenced yard. A fire pit sat beside the piano-shaped pool which took up the rest of the property.

"Nice spot," the man said. "Yours?"

"All mine now."

Emma took a can of maple and bacon-flavored beans down from a shelf and slid it across the kitchen counter toward him. Then she pointed to a drawer. "Can opener and spoon, there."

The man grinned. "You Tarzan. Me, Jane."

"Excuse me? Are you insinuating I've lost some social skills, sir?"

He shrugged. "Haven't we all?"

"I may have shed some of the niceties, but I'm the one feeding you. You look and smell like you haven't had a bath in forever and you're obviously starving."

"Can I have a dip in your pool later?"

"No, that's my drinking water. I'm not drinking your bathwater."

"Sorry. Is drinking pool water safe?"

She bobbed her head. "You have to strain it through clean cloth and boil it, but yeah. I had tablets to purify water a while back. Ran out. If you want to clean up, I'd suggest finding a bar of soap and going for a swim in Klamath Lake."

"Any good fishing around here?"

"Rainbow trout. Same lake."

The man pulled a spoon and the can opener from the kitchen drawer and opened the can of beans. He dug into the cold beans enthusiastically, wolfing down the meal.

"Hey! Whoa, horsie! If you haven't eaten in a while, you'll get cramps if you overwhelm your system all at once."

He nodded his thanks and made a show of chewing slowly.

She remained standing across the room and still held the spear.

"You have nothing to fear from me," he said.

"It didn't occur to me you were a threat."

"Then why the spear?"

"That's one reason you aren't a threat. You said you wanted to see the Pacific before you die. Are you planning to kill yourself in Brookings?"

He chewed and swallowed, seeming to consider his answer for a long time. "It's not suicidal ideation, exactly. It's just, how long can a person be expected to go on? I was in a good place for a while."

"And then?"

"Saw too much."

"Too much death?"

"Too much suffering. I met a woman on my trek through Idaho. Nice person, name of Constance Woodward. Her husband, Cooper, had been a plumber. She'd worked as an operating room nurse for years. Once they retired to take over a little farm, they planned to spend their golden years doing crossword puzzles and raising alpacas. By the time I got there, the animals were all eaten, and Cooper was buried in the backyard, shot in the head for the obvious reason. I rested in Connie's barn for a couple of days and, for the price of a few chores, she fed me. I was just about to be on my way when she asked me to perform one more chore. She asked me to kill her and bury her beside Cooper."

"Was she sick?"

The man shook his head sadly. "Toothache is all it took. Painkillers were barely touching it anymore and it was abscessed. Connie couldn't sleep or eat. If there were a dentist and antibiotics around, Connie would still be working on her big book of crossword puzzles."

"Did you do as she asked?"

"I refused, offered to pull the tooth for her. She said I could help her in the morning. Bright and early the next day, I found her swinging from a rope. I cut her down and had to put a hammer through her skull anyway. I guess she had the last laugh. I did as Connie asked and buried her next to her husband."

Emma took a seat across the room and watched the man eat.

"What about you?" he asked. "Where's your group?"

"Nearby."

"You're alone, aren't you?"

"I am not."

"You don't have to lie. I won't give you any trouble."

"I know you won't."

"Well, okay, then."

The man scraped the liquid from the can of beans until he could scrape no more, and thanked her. "Are there many people left in Klamath Falls? I haven't seen another living soul besides you."

"There might be a few left. I've seen tracks and signs. Guess they're scared and only come out when they have to. Most cleared out after the first winter. We get a lot of sunshine because we're in the high desert, but the snows are heavy."

"I haven't seen any of the dead souls, either," he said.

"We pretty much cleared them out, too."

"Except for that restaurant owner you don't like."

"Like I said, 'Pretty much.'"

The man thanked her for her hospitality, picked up his backpack, and headed for the door. He was halfway there when Emma ran up behind him. He managed a half turn before she struck him in the back of the head with the butt of her spear. She used all the force she could muster. He didn't lose consciousness completely, but his legs had turned to mush, and the pain in his skull blocked out everything else.

Only a few moments passed, but when he got his bearings, he found himself face down on the floor of the foyer. His hands were bound, and when he tried to free himself, something sharp bit into his wrists.

"Zip ties," Emma said. "If you want to piss me off, keep struggling."

He sighed. "If not for that can of beans, I'd be down the road by now."

She circled him twice, picked up his backpack, and rummaged through it.

"Take what you want. It's my canteen, some dirty underwear, toilet paper, a toothbrush, socks, and a compass. There might still be some dust in the Doritos bag. I was going to lick that up for dinner."

Emma didn't believe him at first. When she found he was telling the truth, she took the compass and pocketed it. She considered stealing the canteen, too, but decided she didn't need it. She pulled out the roll of toilet paper and placed it on a shelf. Tossing the backpack aside, she asked, "Why so many socks?"

"Fresh socks get you another five miles of hiking."

Without another word, Emma began dragging him by his feet down the hallway.

"I'll just rest here a bit longer," he said. "If you wanted something, all you had to do was ask. You didn't have to brain me. I've got nothing that's worth adding to the weight of your sins."

"Didn't your mother warn you not to talk to strangers? This is on you."

"Just glad this is a hardwood floor. It would suck to get rug burn on top of a banging headache."

"Not smart, but he's a wise guy," Emma muttered to herself.

She dragged him halfway down the hall to a door and snatched up her spear where she'd dropped it.

"Okay," the man said. "I have questions."

"Don't care. You're about to go down the basement stairs. I can drag you down, and you'll hit your head on every step."

"Or?"

"I can let you up and you can walk. Your choice."

"Walking sounds more civilized. But why do you want a prisoner, miss? I'm skinny, but given a few days, I'll eat you out of house and home."

"You won't be here that long."

"Oh. So ... you gonna help me up?"

"This isn't my first rodeo. Get yourself to your feet."

"With my hands behind my back?"

"You'll figure it out."

It took the man a couple of minutes to roll up to a seated position. Emma waited patiently as he struggled. First, he leaned on the wall and inched up.

"Don't stall or I'll stab you," Emma warned.

"Who's stalling?" He finally got his feet under him and managed to stand. The man looked at her miserably. "My safe word is 'Ow, please stop hurting me.'"

She turned the key to unlock the door to the basement stairs, swung it open, and motioned him down into the dark.

"If you're going to kill me, just do it."

"I'm not a monster," she said. "You do have a purpose."

"Oh, I can't wait to find out what that might be. I never really had one of those before. Even when I thought I did — "

Without warning, she slipped the spear's blade under his throat as she drew the machete from her sash. "This is such a nice house, I'd rather not spend the rest of the day cleaning your blood out of the foyer."

"But you will if you have to. I get it." He edged toward the door and down the stairs. Tiny windows provided dim illumination. The basement was deep and unfinished. With Emma behind him and the spear at his back, they descended into the metallic odor of blood and the stink of shit. A figure at the far end of the basement, little more than a silhouette, let out a low growl.

When the infected killer lunged, chains rattled at his feet. The chains were wrapped and locked around his ankles. Anchored to a metal support post, he was free to move in a circle that was no more than eight feet wide.

The man came to an abrupt halt and only moved forward when Emma pressed the tip of the spear between his shoulder blades.

"What is this?" he asked.

"Not what. Who."

"Or should that be whom? Or whomst? That stuff always confused me."

Showing real anger for the first time, Emma's lip curled. "You think you can joke and charm your way out of this? Like it or not, this is happening. I hate it when people don't take me seriously. You're not the first person I've brought down here."

"I take you very seriously," the man said. "Knew you were trouble from the beginning but there were beans. In retrospect, I should have asked for wieners, too. This wasn't worth the beans. I'd hoped my last meal would be fancier and shared with friends."

"Go," she said. "Feed him." She prodded with the spear again.

"If I'm to die, I want to know why."

"He won't eat canned food. Even a freshly killed rabbit won't quite do. He just pokes at it. He needs fresh meat that's still screaming as he feeds."

"But why? Why haven't you released him?"

"By released, you mean kill."

"It would be a mercy."

"It would be murder."

"And feeding me to him *wouldn't* be?"

"I don't know you. I love him."

"You didn't want to know me. You never even asked my name, and you didn't give me yours."

"I only ask what I need to know."

"It would be nice to know what I'm dying for. Is that your boyfriend, lover, husband, adulterer, or what? If this is a love is blind situation, I can tell you hatred and love can share the same folly. Blind love and blind hatred all ends with somebody not being their best self, and everybody gets to be unhappy."

"He's my brother. He was a doctor, and he worked at the medical center. He worked so hard to help others, my mother called him the Saint."

"He isn't that person anymore."

Emma shoved him toward the zombie. "I know. Of course, I know!"

"Are you waiting for a cure or something? I don't think there's even anyone left working on that!"

"I'm not an idiot."

The man sighed. "What does that leave? Psychopathy?"

"Righteous anger," she said. "The only way I can make the rage a little less potent is by loving my brother. This is how I do it. If I keep him fed, he pretty much looks the same. As long as I keep him ... as long as I have him here, he's not all the way dead."

"Grief sure did a number on you, huh?"

She shrugged. "I'm not so different from before the pandemic. Our mother never called me a saint."

"Miss, we've all done things in the heat of the moment we regret. Believe me, I know from personal experience — "

She gored him in the side with the spear.

The man gasped in pain and surprise before doubling over.

Smelling fresh blood, Emma's brother lunged. His prey stood just out of reach. Frustrated by his restraints, the infected man howled.

"That's blood lust," Emma said. "Ever hear that sound before?"

"I have, yeah."

Emma threw the spear aside and brandished the machete. "Go to him now, or I can hack off an arm, and we can do this a little at a time."

"Like you did with that Clay guy? I'm just trying to understand. Is that how this started for you?"

She pulled the man up by the hair. "This is how it *ends*. Twenty-two thousand people lived in Klamath, and now they're just about all gone. The more people went away, the more peaceful it got around here. I've cut up humans and zombies both. My brother gives me purpose, and I give him food. That's exactly how small and simple I want my world to be."

The man winced. "That's how you quiet the demons, huh?" In great pain and with a hammering heart, he bent forward from the waist again. His breath shallow, the man's voice rose barely above a whisper. "You're an introvert and radically proactive about it. People are gross. I do understand the impulse to isolate."

Emma bent to hear him speak. "What did you say to me?"

He muttered something under his breath, then rose suddenly, ramming the back of his head under her chin. He managed to slip to Emma's side, shouldered her toward her brother, and tripped her as he fell to the concrete floor beside her. Her machete clattered to the floor.

She cursed the man and kicked him in the face. The heel of her right boot caught him with a savage blow just above his left eye.

Emma rose and reached for the machete as the man lay helpless and bleeding at her feet. She would have dismembered him slowly if not for her long ponytail. Her brother reached out, grabbed it, and pulled Emma into his killing circle.

"Kevin! No! No, Kevin!"

As she fought him off, the man rolled toward the machete. In pain and with great difficulty, he managed to grasp the blade and roll back toward safety.

The thick magazines gave Emma a fighting chance. Rather than getting bit, she shoved one armored forearm into her brother's mouth as she struggled to get to her feet.

Desperate to free himself, the man cut the base of his thumb and nicked a couple of fingers as he struggled to cut the zip ties that bound his wrists. With great effort, he managed it. His hands were free, but he was wounded and losing blood.

Frustrated and filled with an undeniable need, the infected man fought with his sister. However, Kevin Dunn had become nothing more than a rabid animal. Emma was stronger and more clever. She forced him back against the support post and drove the heel of her boot into his knee. The joint made a sickening snap, and the zombie went down.

Emma ripped her arm free of her brother's drooling jaws, backed away to safety, and whirled on the man who'd been her prisoner. Her eyes went wide as the man gored her in the stomach with her spear and used the weapon to shove and steer the woman to her doom.

The infected man who had once been Dr. Kevin Dunn sank his teeth into his sister's face. He chewed and ate with feral abandon as she wriggled and screamed.

Wounded and shaking, the man edged toward the stairs as Emma struggled. He could have shown them mercy and stabbed them both to death with the spear. Instead, he climbed the stairs. He got to the top before he stopped to look back at the woman in the clutches of the cannibal killer.

Don't, he thought. *Don't be Do-nothing Nate. Don't be Giddyup Nate, either. Find the middle way. Be your best Nate.*

The man turned around. "My name is Nathaniel Bixby. I used to be an accountant. Then things happened and I did some things I swore I'd never do again."

He descended the stairs and used the spear to give mercy to what was left of the Dunn family of Klamath Falls, Oregon.

WHEN HE GOT back upstairs to the foyer, Nate locked the door behind him. He planned to leave a note warning anyone who might happen on it to refrain from entering the basement. Tearing his shirt open to inspect his belly wound, he found that the spearhead had not penetrated deeply. Relieved he didn't have a perforated bowel, he searched the shelves for first aid supplies. After searching for some time, he found what he needed to clean the wound, seal the edges with glue, and bandage it.

He found no antibiotics among the medical gear, but there were painkillers and an antiseptic spray. Over the next few days, he would check the wound and replace the bandages to keep it clean. It was so hard to stay clean in the apocalypse. The painkillers were long past their best-by date. Nonetheless, he dry swallowed a double dose and hoped the medication wouldn't hurt his stomach lining too much. The beans would help.

She wasn't giving me a last meal out of charity to a condemned man, he thought. *She was just getting me to drop my guard so she could get close enough to knock me over the head.*

Knowing he'd come so close to getting eaten alive made him shiver with revulsion. With some difficulty, Nate climbed the stairs and found an empty bedroom. Glancing in a mirror, he realized that he'd neglected to bandage the wound above his eye where Emma had kicked him. The cut at the base of his thumb was still bleeding a little. However, his headache was so intense, he couldn't be bothered to deal with it right away. Instead, he climbed into bed and fell asleep immediately.

If I don't ever wake up, he thought, *I'll know she gave me a hairline skull fracture. If there's not enough brain swelling and blood sloshing around inside my head, ol' Clay the former restaurateur might get some company. I don't want to be zombie buddies, but right now, all I want to do is sleep.*

When he awoke, it was dark. His watch had died long ago, but that mattered little. Since Vegas, he'd met few people. No more were there times when other people's expectations had to be met. Without a schedule, each day was simpler. His life was not broken into hours and minutes anymore. There was dawn and dusk. The only other significant time increments were the answer to the questions: When did he last eat? When would he eat again?

Reluctantly, he hauled himself up from the bed and made his way to a balcony at the front of the house. As he urinated off the balcony into the front yard, Nate planned his next steps.

At daylight, he would find what Emma used for a bathroom. He hoped she hadn't used the basement. No power on Earth could make him go down there again. With her latrine located and so few people around, staying in Klamath Falls was his safest bet.

But he'd heard about Brookings' beaches from Cheryl. She had grown up there. In his fantasy, a friendly survivalist community waited for him. He would somehow find her parents' house, and there would be old albums full of pictures of her as a little girl. Maybe some of her relatives would still be alive, and he could make up for his sins by taking care of them.

He almost laughed at himself. There was no such thing as a friendly survivalist community. People were scared and no one liked being scared, so instead, they got angry.

There's hardly a crack of light between me and my captor, he thought. *She just stayed angry at the world longer. If I still had the energy, I'd be pissed off, too.*

The next day, Nate took a full inventory of Emma's stores. In his rush to find a first aid kit, he'd thrown some stuff on the floor. He grunted in pain as he bent over to put cans of food back on the shelf.

Taking over her tiny empire is going to have to wait, he thought. *I gotta take this slow.*

Nate rested another day before daring to explore the neighborhood. He found fishing gear in the garage and was eager to pull a couple of rainbow trout from the lake. On the way, he passed Clay Filmore. The chained zombie growled at him, and Nate gave him a nod. "Don't mind me, sir! It's been a long time since I've been on vacation. I won't bother you."

He got a nibble on the first cast and then nothing for an hour. He couldn't recall visiting a place that was so small yet called itself a city. "Rural city" seemed like an oxymoron, yet here he was, sitting by a lake without another living soul around for miles, at least, as far as he could tell. He kept the spear by his side, but nothing bothered him except a persistent headache, his aching wound, and a couple of crows who wanted his lunch.

If a can of sardines is all I get for sitting out here in the sun all day, it still wouldn't be half bad.

By mid-afternoon, he still hadn't caught a single rainbow trout, but the three white bass he'd caught would make a fine feast. He decided to try again the next day. Nate considered the possibility he was using the wrong bait. As he passed Clay Filmore on the way back, he asked, "You think worms would be better? If my dad were here, he'd say big red wigglers are the best for any fish you'd actually want to eat."

The zombie growled and lunged. The chain snapped his head backward.

"You're starving, you don't learn, and you're a lousy conversationalist. That's just cruel, isn't it?" Nate sighed. "You know I'm on vacation, right?"

The limbless corpse regarded him with eyes like nailheads and bared his rotting teeth.

Nate put down the fishing gear and the pail carrying the three fish. As he walked closer, the zombie lunged again. He came for him with the spear. With one hard thrust that made Nate's wounded torso burn, he ended Clay Filmore's misery.

"Mercy for you," Nate said. "I hope that earns a little mercy for me."

After a few more days, Nate considered moving on. He did not believe in ghosts, but the curse of memory was enough to make the house feel haunted. He could have simply relocated down the road, but he was living in a ghost town. When he closed his eyes, he could still picture the look of surprise on Emma's face when he stabbed her in the stomach and pushed her to her death. He may as well have pushed her off a cliff. That would have been kinder.

Sometimes, he would pause at the basement door and listen for movement. He turned the knob at least a couple of times a day, not to open it, but to confirm that the door was still locked.

Nate found himself apologizing to Emma despite everything. "In a disease-free world, your brother would still be a doctor. You tried to murder me and that's not okay. However, in a better world, you would have gotten meds, counseling, and maybe a straitjacket. You deserved better, but what can I tell you? Trauma does things to people."

Choosing food carefully from Emma's stores, he loaded a little wagon gardeners used for yard waste. Pulling it on a rope tied around his waist, all Nate had to do was oil the wheels so they wouldn't squeak. He couldn't take a plane to Brookings, but if his luck held out, he could fly below the radar. Klamath Falls was so eerily quiet, he felt as if he were the last man on Earth. As a precaution, he took Emma's spear anyway.

For two days, Nate trekked west and he felt fine. On the third day, he began getting stomach cramps. He thought his wound might be the culprit, but it seemed to be healing as expected. Nate wanted to ascribe the discomfort to food poisoning. That didn't really fit, either.

On the fourth day, his jaw began to cramp. He rested more frequently, but spent longer hours on the road, determined to make it to the Pacific. Pain and stiffness took over every muscle in his body. By the time he got to the sign welcoming him to the outskirts of Brookings, he felt like an old man who'd been beaten with heavy sticks.

With every step through the town, his head became a pounding drum. He was too hot and couldn't cool down. Somewhere in the middle of Brookings, he left his wagon behind and did not look back. There was only one mission now. He had to get to the ocean.

"From the ocean, we emerged, and to the ocean, I shall return."

Slick with sweat, Nate stepped onto Lone Ranch Beach. Exhausted and sick, he pulled off his shoes and dropped. The sand felt good between his toes. Best of all, it was wonderful to finally give up running from Death.

If the Reaper wants to meet me here, he thought, *I'll keep the appointment.*

Nate had not seen another human being nor another of the infected since he killed Clay Filmore.

No, I did not kill a man. I killed whatever was left of him. I ended the husk that was chained up and forgot to lie down and die. No sense adding to my sins. I've got enough to be sorry for already.

Looking around the deserted beach, only birds remained. If he'd had the energy to dig, he fantasized about building a fire and having a clambake. He imagined Cheryl had played on this same beach as a girl.

The spasms in his jaw hit hard, and Nate had to lie back and close his eyes against the pain. He could not have opened his mouth wide enough to cram in a toothbrush. Helpless, all he could do was wait for the suffering to pass.

Jaw cramps. That triggered a memory. He was not infected, at least not with RABID-24. He peeled back the small bandage from the base of his thumb. It didn't look remarkable except for some redness around the edges, but Nate was almost sure of the reason for his aches, pains, fever, and chills.

Jaw cramping was the telltale sign. His fevered brain served up a dim memory of a cartoon from a Boy Scout handbook. The image was of an old man with his jaw wrapped in a bandage and stars circling his head that were supposed to indicate pain. The caption read: *Beware of rusty nails! Get your tetanus shot!*

The rusty machete that freed him from Emma's zip ties had also condemned him to death. It wasn't the rust that would soon send him into deadly seizures. It was the bacteria concealed in the dirty blade.

He lay in the warm and welcoming sand, crying. The jaw cramping slowly eased, but the fever did not.

Staring up at the clear azure sky, he managed to let out a chuckle. *I haven't seen another human for days. No zombies, either. I could have gone to sleep tonight dreaming that the Ragin' Contagion was finally really over. The disease that's wiping out my species didn't get me, but there's still plenty else to die from.*

When he spoke, he discovered he had trouble swallowing. "I don't deserve this, but, since Cheryl, I don't *not* deserve this, either. Seems like we're always worried about the wrong thing, and what gets you in the end is a surprise. You have to get very near the end before you start conceding that you aren't immortal."

As a warm breeze slipped over him, Nate wished he could tell Cheryl she was right. The Pacific was as lovely on a sunny day as she'd once described.

Sorry about Vegas, Cheryl. Less sorry about Jayden, but still sorry.

The sky was so clear of clouds, he hoped to see the stars before he died, but night was far away, and Death was closing in.

When he was a little boy, he'd fantasized that he was being watched by vague benevolent forces. Certain he was bound for great things, someone had to be watching. His father had believed in a giving and forgiving god until his wife was on her deathbed. When his prayers for her recovery came to nothing, his dad never went to church again.

Somehow, some small part of Nate had held to the fantasy that he was important, that there was justice, and he would be rewarded. On that beach in Brookings, Oregon, he found his fate, and with that, clarity.

The waves will continue. The sun will rise without me.

The sun set as Nate Bixby muttered his last, "Everyone thinks they'll survive whatever comes, that suffering and dying is only for others. The horror isn't in what's happened. What's really scary is that the universe is so indifferent."

PROMISES

The last of dusk's long shadows closed over Mira Langley like cold fingers as she walked down the old trail into the ghost town. She wanted to call out to her son, but she didn't dare stir the last of the town's residents. If they knew she was there, they would attack. If they'd caught Tyler, her twelve-year-old was already dead.

All the windows along the street had been smashed long ago. Peering in storefront after storefront, everything useful appeared to have been looted. The little grocery store's shelves had been emptied completely.

Hearing a faint noise, she paused by a novelty shop to find that Halloween decorations were still hung in the display. A robin's nest sat in the corner, but it seemed even the birds had abandoned the town.

I can understand looting the grocery and hardware stores, she thought, *but what was gained smashing the window to a place selling plastic skeletons, geegaws, and fireworks? We've got quite enough of the real skeletons.*

In a stage whisper, she called through the open window, "Tyler? Are you in there?"

Someone did reply, but it wasn't Tyler. An irritated man with a high voice answered, "What are you doing?"

"Hello?"

A thin man of about sixty stepped out of the darkness at the rear of the store and tiptoed forward. His face and white hair were flecked with what looked like fresh blood. His shirt, pants, and boots were dark with old blood, the color of rust. The mallet clenched in his right hand dripped with blood. The man's words were rushed but remained hushed. "Let me clue you in, lady. This is a big game of hide and seek. This is my hiding spot. *Mine*, understand? Go find your own."

Mira drew her sawed-off shotgun from the holster rig beneath her backpack. "Let me clue you in. I'm looking for my son. He's twelve and the last anybody saw of him, he was headed this way."

Staring down her weapon's double-barrel, the man appeared to deflate. "No need for that. You fire that thing, you'll bring them for both of us."

"Well, it wouldn't really be for *both* of us, would it?"

"Who are you?"

"Mira. I'm the sheriff in Hood River."

"Sheriff, huh? What happened to the old one, the guy who took over after the revolution?"

"That was two sheriffs ago. Sheriff Crane was elected after the revolution, and Sheriff Tiegs took over after secession."

"I knew Tiegs. He grew up, born and raised in Wasco County. What happened to him?"

"I'm sure you can guess."

"And what's happening in Hood River now?"

"Chaos. We had an outbreak after one of our elders passed away. He was a loner, so no one got to him in time."

The man bobbed his head. "And what makes you think your son is still alive? How do you know he's not out on the 84?"

"He was last seen headed this way on the trails. To avoid being an easy target, he'd know to stay off the Columbia River Highway. We always said that in case of an outbreak, Mosier would be where we'd meet up if we were separated. There's nothing else around for miles, so here I am, asking you politely for your help. I've been patient, bringing you all the news of the world. I'm out of patience, and in a minute, I won't be so polite." Mira cocked the shotgun.

"I don't know what you expect of me. I ain't seen your boy."

"Mosier's small. He'll appear. That's why we chose it as a rendezvous point."

The man shook his head doubtfully. "Lot to expect of a twelve-year-old, don't you think?"

"Twelve isn't what it used to be, mister."

"Why don't you calm down and point your little boomstick in another direction?"

"Not before you tell me what that's all about." She nodded to the mallet in his hand.

He grinned. "There's a horde nearby. I spotted a passel of 'em the other day, up on the cliffs, staggerin' around in circles. Some of the stragglers wandered off and found their way into town. I snuck up on one and took him down. Can't be too careful."

The blood in his hair was still wet and some on his cheek was freshly smeared in a hurried attempt to wipe it away. Mira lowered the shotgun's muzzle. His smile quickly faded when he realized she was pointing it at his crotch.

"Drop the weapon," she said.

The mallet hit the linoleum with a heavy clunk.

"Hands behind your head and step back. I'm coming through the door, and you better not move."

The man kept his hands at his sides.

"Do as you're told!"

"My name is Derek Chesley, and I've lived in Mosier all my life. I worked at the sewage treatment plant. I was here for the train derailment in 2016, saw it happen with my own eyes. I helped fight the fires in 2020. I don't know much, but I know you're not sheriff here. You got no authority. You lost your boy, now you've lost your damn mind. Gun or not, you will not control me. Now, settle down, hear?"

Chesley bent to pick up the mallet.

"Don't test me!" Mira yelled.

From the dark recesses at the rear of the store, a woman screamed. "Is someone there? Help! Help me, please! He's going to kill me!"

Mira rushed through the shattered front door. Chesley cocked his arm, ready to throw the mallet at her face. She pulled the trigger. In the small space, the shotgun's report sounded like a cannon.

Derek Chesley went down as if his knees were made of hot wax. Blood poured from the wound in his belly. Mira froze for a moment. As her ears rang with a high whine, she watched a pool of blood creep across the floor toward her.

Chesley looked up at her. "You hadn't oughta do that. I was just kiddin' around ... *oooh* ... that smarts. I was just kiddin'."

"I wasn't," Mira told him.

"You better finish me off!" he pleaded. "Don't let me become one of them!"

She left him to check the back of the store. Pulling a small flashlight from her belt, Mira shot the beam into the darkness.

"Help! Help! Did you get him? Please, God, help me!"

Behind a little checkout counter, Mira found a door disguised as a shelving unit laden with cheap non-stick muffin trays and party supplies. Mira slipped to the side of the door and listened. All she could hear was the woman pleading to be set free.

"Who's in there?"

There was a moment's hesitation. Her ears still rang, but at the edge of perception, Mira thought she heard another voice. She couldn't make out the words, but the tone was wrong.

"It's just me! Alice! I'm Alice Hardaway!"

Mira straightened in surprise. She knew that name. Alice was one of the more elderly of Hood River's 248 survivors.

Scratch that, Mira thought. *Only God or the Devil knew how many of Hood Rover's citizens were left alive now.*

"I'll just be a minute, Mrs. Hardaway!"

"*What?*"

"I'll be right back!"

"Wait! Don't leave me! Don't leave me here, you heartless bitch!"

Mira stalked back to Derek Chesley. "Who's in there with her?"

Covered in blood, the man looked up at her helplessly. His breathing was already short. He panted, "I'm trying ... to hold ... my ... my ... guts in."

Mira dug a shotgun cartridge out of her vest pocket and replaced the spent shell.

"Tell me how many are back there, or I *won't* shoot you in the head. I'll leave you to turn. Maybe you'll join the horde, make new friends, and finally find out what goes on in a monster's mind. We've always wondered."

"You ... wouldn't. It ain't ... natural."

"You don't have any time to negotiate. I already told you once not to test me."

Derek Chesley wept. "Lyle. My brother ... back there with her."

"Armed?"

When he said nothing, she placed her weapon's muzzle against his knee. "It'll hurt more than getting shot in the crotch, probably. I've got two shells to spare, so maybe with your dying breath you can tell me yourself which wound delivers the most agony per square inch."

"He's got a 30-06," he admitted. "Don't ... hurt him."

"I promise I won't."

Mira stalked back to the rear of the store, taking deep breaths, and trying to calm her pounding heart. Slipping to the side of the door again, she reached out and tested the knob. It would not turn.

The worst of the ringing in her ears had ebbed. She heard a male voice say something she couldn't decipher. The tone was angry.

"I need help! What's going on out there?" Alice yelled.

"Try to relax, Alice. The door won't open, and Mr. Chesley says he doesn't have a key. I've got a hairpin. I'm going to pick the lock, and I'll have you out in a few minutes."

Mira stayed to the side of the door, straining to hear what might be said.

"Are you working the lock?" Alice asked.

"Yup! Just a sec!"

With a great boom, a bullet ripped through the front of the door just below the doorknob. The door burst open, and a tall skinny man stepped through. He expected to find Mira on the floor bleeding to death. Instead, she stuck the muzzle in his ribs and pulled the trigger. The shotgun's blast was muffled by Lyle Chesley's body.

The rifle clattered to the floor and slid away as the man dropped and writhed in pain.

Derek called out to his brother. "Lyle? You ... okay?"

"He's not!" Mira yelled.

Ignoring the Chesley brothers, Mira checked her angles around the door. The back room was larger than she expected. Rather than finding a stockroom, she discovered a one-room apartment. A dirty window at the rear of the building yielded a dim rectangle of light from the dying day. So far, it was the only glass window Mira had seen in town that remained unbroken.

A hissing kerosene lamp provided most of the room's illumination. The lamp sat beside Alice Hardaway, revealing her haggard and terrified visage. Tears slipped down her wrinkled cheeks.

Beside her lay a body Mira recognized as Alice's husband Craig. His skull had been bashed in, and the floor was awash in blood. Mira had interrupted a crime, but she was too late for Craig Hardaway.

Alice's hands were tied with electrical cord. Mira pulled a knife from her belt and cut through it. As soon as the old woman was free, she got to her feet stiffly. She turned and hugged her rescuer. "Thank you! Thank you, Sheriff! They were going to eat us!"

After a few seconds, Alice turned to her husband's corpse, but Mira pulled her away, unwilling to allow the widow to linger. "We've been making a lot of noise. If there are any of the *other* kind of cannibals around, they'll be coming."

"But, Craig!"

"I'm sorry, your husband is beyond help, and my son is missing. I have to find Tyler."

When Mira turned, she found Derek crawling toward his dying brother. Gasping and wincing in pain, he'd left a blood trail down the fireworks aisle. Even in the dim light, both brothers had lost so much blood, their skin had turned gray. They didn't have long.

Mira stalked over to the rifle Lyle dropped and handed it to the old woman.

Derek looked up at her miserably. "You said you wouldn't hurt him."

"Couldn't be helped," Mira replied. "I didn't mean to hurt your brother. I meant to kill him. Soon enough, he'll be gone."

"And then he'll come back," Alice said. "We should ... "

The old woman pointed the 30-06 at Lyle's head, but Mira stopped her. "I have a more elegant solution that won't waste bullets."

Derek reached out and brushed his brother's hair from his eyes. "I'm sorry, Lyle. So sorry. I should have ... shoulda looked out for you ... better."

"It's not enough that the zombies eat us and infect us? We have to worry about people like you, too?" Alice demanded. The old woman grabbed a dirty blanket off a narrow bed and covered her fallen husband.

Mira searched the one-room apartment briefly, but found no food, ammunition, or other weapons. She bent to check Lyle's pockets and found a box of rounds. To her disappointment, the box of 30-06 ammunition was light and rattled, obviously near empty.

The sheriff stepped over Lyle and went down a different aisle to avoid slipping in Derek's trail of blood. In a moment, she was back, mallet in hand. As she stood over the brothers, Derek's eyes widened.

"You ... you have another promise ... to keep. Kill me. If you ... if you won't waste ... a bullet, kill me like ... like I killed the old man. Make it quick."

Mira dropped the mallet beside him. "Do it yourself. You should kill your brother first. If he turns and you're too weak to cave in your own skull, well ... there you go."

For a moment, Mira thought Alice would object. Then she thought the old woman might shoot the brothers to avenge her husband. Instead, she muttered, "I'm a tough old bird. Barely enough meat on my bones to feed the two of you. If Craig were alive, he'd call you both rascals, *awful* rascals! But my man has gone on to his reward. And you?" She pointed to the bloody mallet. "That's your reward. Sheriff? Can we go now?"

Mira was almost out the front door when she doubled back and grabbed two long boxes of fireworks.

"What are we celebrating?" Alice asked.

"My kid is missing and it's almost dark. I know how much he loves fireworks. Mosier is small enough, maybe I can get his attention."

"Those will attract the monsters, too, though."

"I haven't worked that out in my head yet. Gimme time."

Alice had not been wrong about attracting the wrong kind of attention. They already had. Down the street, Mira counted seven zombies lurching toward them. Then two more emerged from the parking lot beside the novelty shop.

Alice cursed, crossed herself, and began to pray. "You should know, with my knees, I'm not much of a runner, Sheriff."

"I have an idea." Mira pulled Alice back into the shop and grabbed a roll of duct tape from a hook on the wall display. A box of lighters sat by the cash register at the back, and Mira grabbed a handful of those as well.

Derek had not touched the mallet that lay beside him. He looked almost relieved to see the pair. Wincing in pain, he managed to say, "Forget something?"

"Just passing through!"

"I'm cold," Derek said. "I'm ...really cold."

"That must be very difficult for you," Alice observed. "Almost as bad as getting tied to a chair and watching a couple of psychopaths bludgeon your spouse, knowing you're next."

"Sorry," Derek mumbled.

"I accept your apology," the old woman said, "but only because it won't do you any good."

Suddenly inspired, Mira grabbed a stuffed teddy bear from a shelf. "You're going to want to take me up on my first offer and use that mallet," she told Derek. "The backup plan is going to suck for you."

They stepped around the pair of dying brothers and reentered the apartment. "Leave the door open, Alice!"

"*Sh!* They'll hear you!"

"That's kind of the idea."

They had been followed into the shop. The zombies had spotted Mira and Alice, and that brought them to the front door. The aroma of freshly spilled blood was enough to lure the town's invaders in toward the back.

Lyle still lay unconscious. Derek found enough lung capacity to give a weak yelp as, with trembling and clumsy hands, he scrambled for the mallet.

Deft with her knife, Mira cut into the box of fireworks.

"They're coming!" Alice warned.

"Yes, time is a factor," Mira admitted. "There will be no leisurely reading of the instructions, and the little red schoolhouse firework isn't going to be much help. Open that other box, quick!" She handed Alice the knife and tore through the contents of the box she'd opened.

Spinners, sparklers, and poppers wouldn't serve Mira's purpose, but the firecrackers and the bottle rockets might. Alice struggled to get her box open, but finally managed it.

"Forget that, hold this." Mira held out the teddy bear.

The old woman did as she was told but looked mystified as Mira wrapped firecrackers around the body of the stuffed toy.

"What?" Mira asked. "You didn't have a misspent youth setting Barbies on fire and such?"

Low growls could be heard coming from the front of the store. Derek had gone quiet, but he was still conscious and clutching his mallet to his chest.

As Alice peered through the door, Derek looked over at her with pleading eyes and mouthed the words, "Kill me."

Alice mouthed back, "Pig."

More zombies entered the store and shambled down the narrow aisles, knocking over displays as they advanced.

"More cannibal killers are being added to our collection, Sheriff," Alice whispered. "Whatever you're going to do, I wish you'd do it."

As she finished taping two strands of firecrackers around the teddy bear, Mira ordered Alice to open the apartment's rear window.

The zombies were almost upon the brothers when Lyle awoke. The man's eyes popped open so wide, even in the dim light, Mira could see the whites of his eyes all around his tiny pupils.

No, no longer a man, Mira thought. *He's one of them.*

"Lyle?" Derek asked. "It's me. It's ... your big brother."

The thing that had been Lyle Chesley crawled forward and dove into his brother's wet abdominal wound. The invaders converged on Derek as he attempted to use the mallet on his brother's skull. He was too weak to do much damage to his brother, and he was far too late to attempt to use the mallet on himself. In the end, the murderer wasn't even strong enough to let out a scream of anguish or pain.

Behind her, Alice said, "Enjoy the buffet, you filthy abominations."

Mira's stomach turned as, with shaking hands, she lit the firecracker strand. She tossed it through the door and among the scrabbling vultures clawing at Derek Chesley's body. The strand began popping as it landed atop the Chesley brothers, and among the newly arrived zombies.

As the teddy bear exploded into flames, Mira grabbed rockets from the box and fired them through the open door.

Alice appeared by her side. "What are you doing?"

"Not sure! I've never fired rockets indoors before!"

"Fireworks won't kill them!"

Mira did not stop grabbing rockets, flicking a lighter, and shooting them out into the store. "I'm not trying to kill them exactly. First priority is to light this place on fire!"

"Oh." Alice disappeared behind her. Mira assumed the old woman was headed for the window to escape. Instead, she got down on her knees and smashed the box of disposable lighters with the butt of the rifle. The plastic cracked easily to release the lighter fluid.

"Good idea!" Mira grabbed the box and tossed it amid all the fireworks she'd already thrown. A fire had already begun. When the lighter fluid hit the flames of the burning teddy bear, bright orange light illuminated the shop as the fire built to a roar.

As the zombies' shadows played over them, Mira glimpsed the Chesley brothers one last time. Ignoring the growing heat, and the fact that he was alight, Lyle was still eating. Derek's eyes were rolled up in his head. A cannibal bent as if to kiss him. Instead, the revenant pulled the dead man's lower lip away to chew with apparent relish.

Before the rest of the zombies turned her way, Mira slammed the door shut. Alice stepped over the body of her husband to shove the back of a chair under the doorknob.

"You're useful to have around, Alice," Mira said.

"No flies on me yet, Sheriff. Now, can we please get the hell out of here? I need to go somewhere private to cry for a few weeks."

Mira went out the window first. Alice handed her the rifle. As the sheriff helped the old woman through the window, smoke poured from the shop, and a cacophony of explosions boomed and crackled.

"Got to the rest of the fireworks," Mira said.

"Flammable stuff," Alice muttered. "That's going to spread. I don't imagine there are any firefighters left in this husk of a town."

Ghost town, Mira thought. *Didn't really mean to, but I added to the number of ghosts in Mosier.*

"Glad we're out of there," Alice continued. "*I'm* flammable, too. One blessing: Craig always asked that he be cremated. My husband hated the idea of going down into the cold, cold ground with all the grubs and worms getting at him."

As they retreated, the fire ate its way through the roof. When the firework explosions petered out, the whole structure became engulfed in flames.

"He should have used that mallet on himself right away," Alice said.

Mira took a deep breath and let it out slowly. "That's cold, but yeah."

"You okay, dear?"

"I just killed two men, Alice, so ... no."

"You didn't do a bad thing, Sheriff," the old woman assured her. "Contrary to what some would have you believe, not everybody is of the same worth."

As the pair escaped to the street, Mira froze. One lone figure stood in the street staring at the burning store. It was a small, slim silhouette against the bright flames.

Mira broke into a run. "Tyler!"

The boy turned slowly, and for a long moment, Mira feared the worst. *If my son is a zombie, I want to be one, too,* she thought.

The boy ran at her. "Mom!"

Tyler leaped into his mother's arms, and she swung him around in a circle.

"You've been off on an adventure, boy," Alice said.

Mira grabbed her son by the shoulders, looked at him, then ran her fingers through his thick mop of hair. Tears sprung to her eyes. "Are you hurt at all? When the outbreak hit Hood River, everything got so crazy. I thought I'd lost you!"

"I'm okay, Mom. I didn't get bit. Can we go home now?"

"I'm afraid not. The outbreak ... it spread fast. I don't know how many people got bit before the alarm was even raised, but Hood River is not safe. When the attack hit, I headed straight home. Sally told me she saw you headed for the hills."

"Yeah, I heard the fire hall's alarm, so I bugged out just like you told me."

"Technically, I abandoned my post, but I'm not interested in being the third Hood River sheriff to die in the zombie apocalypse. Looks like I'm out of a job, buddy."

"Where are we going to go?" Tyler asked.

"I had a couple of friends who moved to Maupin. Before communications went out, I talked to them a few times a year. That's my best guess as to where to start."

"Do they have kids?"

"I don't know. Let's not get ahead of ourselves, okay? One disaster at a time."

Alice cleared her throat. "That's a good boy you got there."

"Tyler? Do you know Mrs. Hardaway?"

"I've seen her around, maybe."

"Say hello. Then we have to find a place to camp for the night that isn't on fire."

But that was not to be. Derek Chesley had been correct. A horde was nearby, nearer than Mira had imagined. Attracted by the fire and explosions, a mob of zombies came into view down the street.

Mira grabbed her son and started in the opposite direction. Alice trailed behind. Within a hundred yards, the old woman was out of breath. She turned, raised the deer rifle, and fired into the advancing mob.

"Head shots!" Mira told her. "Head shots only!"

"If it weren't so dark, maybe," Alice complained. "I can't even see the sights on the gun!"

Wild-eyed, Tyler seemed on the edge of panic. "If we make it to the woods, can we lose them, Mom?"

Alice took off after the mother and son again. "Can't stay here. The whole town will be on fire before the night's over."

"We can't hole up and wait. They'll track us even easier if we wait for daylight."

"C'mon!" The boy ran ahead, and Mira ran after him. As they hit the edge of town, the advancing darkness hampered their progress.

"Tyler! You've got to slow down!" Mira warned. "If we twist an ankle here, they'll get us!"

Alice trailed them, managing to keep mother and son in sight. The zombies tracked the old woman. Stirred to a frenzy, the freshest and fastest of the monsters were gaining.

Tyler paused to look back at the mob and stared. With spreading fire behind them, their pursuers were just moving shapes, predatory silhouettes that left the horrors of their wounds and decay to the imagination. Tyler was one of those little boys with a very active imagination. The walls of his bedroom back in Hood River were decorated with his artwork: desiccated zombies rising from the grave. As the terrors that haunted his nightmares advanced, his worst imaginings were made real. He cried out, "Mom! What are we going to do?"

She whirled, gauging distances. The woods, the hills, and the uneven ground would slow the trio, but they'd be easier to track if they stuck to the road. Mira could not risk getting into an endurance competition with indefatigable killers.

"I won't let them get you, Tyler. Keep going straight. I'll be right behind you."

Tyler plunged into the forest's darkness.

Mira doubled back to Alice.

Her narrow chest heaving, the old woman puffed, "What's the plan?"

Mira pulled the rifle from Alice's grasp. "I rescued you."

"Yes?"

"You owe me."

"Oh."

"You said not everyone's life is worth the same."

"Ah." The old woman nodded. "You'll have to be quick. Like I told those other fellas, not a lot of meat on my bones. I'll feed them, but not for long."

"Stick to the road. Draw them away."

"Because they'll go for easier, slower prey," Alice said.

"I'm just trying to save my son."

As she ran for her life, Mira heard the old lady call after her, "You did say I was useful to have around!"

LATER, as the sun rose over the Columbia River, the water sparkled. The new day's air was so fresh, it was as if all the horrors of the previous night were erased. People died horribly and the world spun on. But Mira could not move on. Alice's face haunted her.

Given time, I think you would have forgiven me, Mira thought. *Doesn't matter. I cannot forgive myself.*

There was nothing for Mira and Tyler in Maupin. The town had burned down sometime in the distant past, and nothing was left but ashes. Mira didn't know what had happened to her friends but she could guess.

In Shaniko, they found a large camp of survivors and stayed with them for a couple of years. The people were embittered and gruff. Finding enough sustenance for such a large group proved difficult and led to fights, several murders, and suicides. Ironically, the camp's violent deaths eventually led to a solution to the food shortage. They did not resort to cannibalism. There were simply fewer mouths to feed because people had either died or moved on.

On his sixteenth birthday, Tyler announced that he was moving into his own tent with a girl one year his senior. Mira tried to dissuade him, and by the end of that squabble, she had to admit she'd only succeeded in driving her son into his girlfriend's arms.

Tyler was not forgiving. When it became clear her son would never forgive her, anger and self-loathing set in. Meanness seeped into her marrow.

One day, a woman on a motorcycle came through Shaniko on her way to Antelope. Acting on impulse, Mira grabbed her go-bag and her bedroll and asked for a ride.

In Antelope, she struck up a conversation with an elderly couple from Las Vegas. They'd been to the coast and had just enough fuel and friends along the way to get home.

"I've never been to Vegas," Mira said.

"One day, soon, I think, the disease will play itself out," the old man said. "Then we'll go back into the city and make it like it was, only better because we'll be wiser."

"Wiser? I haven't seen much evidence of that," Mira replied.

The old woman beside him cradling an Uzi in her lap smiled. "You have to keep the faith. Maybe you just haven't met the right people yet."

"Maybe," Mira admitted. "Not a lot of hope and faith around here that I can see."

"Then what's keeping you here, girl?"

Mira shrugged. "I guess ... nothing anymore."

"So? Wanna hitch a ride to Vegas and see if the world treats you better?" the old man said. "I promise, we don't bite."

They were old, but somehow through it all, they'd managed to remain kind. Mira wondered how the pair had managed that feat. Was their sunny optimism born of genetics? Was it luck or a character trait that could be developed? Perhaps they only seemed to cling to hope out of a grim determination they masked well.

If I get old, I'll have wrinkles from all the regret and worry, Mira thought. *But this beautiful old soul doesn't really have wrinkles. She has plenty of laugh lines, though. Could I learn how to be like that? I have to know.*

Mira accepted their invitation, climbing aboard their RV before she could change her mind. The old woman put down her machine gun and extended her tiny hand. "I'm Mary and that's John. What's your handle, honey?"

"Cheryl," Mira said. "My name is Cheryl."

DEATH SQUAD

The newest recruits were agile and quick but unseasoned and excitable. As we approached the encampment in the valley, the youngest ones hurried ahead, making too much noise as they crashed through dry brush. I worried they would alert the enemy, give away our position, and foil our attack before it even began.

One of our scouts had spotted their fire from the hills above. We entered the village from the north, exiting the tree line just before dawn. The aroma of cooked meat lingered over the smoldering cooking pit, leading us straight to them. With senses honed by hunger, we made a beeline for the tents.

I'd been injured in the earliest days of the war. The pain was gone, but my left leg still didn't work quite right. I limped forward, falling behind the others. As the oldest soldier in the squad, my forte was not found in running. However, I was still among the largest, and no one dared to begrudge me my share when the spoils were divided.

The smart soldier doesn't only look for what is present, but for what is missing. Experience, often known as failure, taught me to be wary. I scanned the terrain for trip wires, dogs, and guards. No guard dogs raised the alarm as we drew closer. I wondered if the enemy had eaten all their pets. Survival canceled out sentimentality.

Feelings and thoughts led to hesitation, a luxury no one could afford. Hardened by loss and harsh conditions, we no longer suffered such disadvantages. Drained of weakness, Nature had made us a formidable force despite our loss of technology.

In the beginning, the enemy encampments were bigger and better organized. Early on, I'd seen moose and deer bones in cooking pits. Once I'd even seen a bear skinned and butchered to feed a couple of dozen villagers. However, the enemy's hunting grounds had been made sparse. Our opponents' numbers had dwindled, and they had fewer bullets, too.

Some young fool took point and let out a war cry as he burst into the first tent. If he'd remained quiet, we could have waded in among the enemy while they were still groggy. In his excitement, that one member of our squad gave up our best tactical advantage: surprise. As the fresh recruit burst into the tent, a woman's screams alerted the whole camp.

Slowed by age and injury, I was spared the first of the counterattack. Perhaps the enemy had been expecting us, or maybe they were simply quick on their feet. These were not farmers made soft by hiding out in a forgotten valley away from the fray. These were hunters who'd come up against forces such as mine and knew some tricks.

Three of my squad blundered into the main tent and were attacked from all sides by young men with long knives. As my people attacked, spry young people leaped behind my soldiers and slashed their Achilles tendons. My squad bleated like slaughtered lambs as the enemy surrounded them with sharpened poles, stabbing and beating them until they lay still.

I did not mourn them. The heat of battle leaves no time for such dramatics. The relentless weariness of our circumstances left me with no spare energy. However, I did wonder if that was the day we'd finally find ourselves in their cooking pits. Before the sun rose to its full strength, I was sure most of us would be no more, finally at rest and on the menu. They'd turn us on spits to fill their bellies. If they had any salt left, perhaps they'd dry us in the hot sun to preserve us. Maybe they'd put what could be salvaged in brine. If I ended up in a jar, would I know it? Would I care? I had no answers.

Because I understood their hunger, I did not resent their success. I hurried forward. My people needed all the strength I had left. The main tent was a trap, so I kept to the open.

A fierce young girl with a dirty face came at me with a long spear. Her pigtails triggered a memory from before the war. I lunged at her, but part of me was elsewhere. I think I once stood in a city park, and a child I cared about, another little girl in pigtails, stood beside me.

Children are always the most vulnerable when chaos reigns. My attacker looked a little younger than the girl I pictured in the park.

As I grabbed the spear's shaft, I remembered more details. It seemed eons had passed since we'd been separated. She was my daughter. She'd become infected at school so their school gymnasium became a quarantine center.

My wife May had been a nurse. She volunteered to work with those kids in isolation. She walked into the school and never came out. Forgetting can be a gift. I didn't want to know what end my wife suffered.

My duty required me to guard that school, my family's prison, as it burned. As the elementary school turned to smoke and ash, I wept. My orders were to shoot anyone tempted to run into the flames. No one tried to rescue the infected, but I did have to open fire on a few of those who attempted to escape the conflagration.

Another soldier assured me that the smoke would take my family before the fire got a chance to eat, swallow, and digest them. When the structure fell in on itself, I heard screams. My squad told me I was mistaken. They lied, of course, but I appreciated their attempt to spare me.

My CO's face was stone when I confessed my heartbreak. He told me, "Once they walked in, they were never walking out. You're not special, sergeant. I'm not telling you to get over it, but you could spare us and get over yourself. We're all hurting. This is what it is. It's not personal. It's the cost of doing business."

Heavy grief was not made lighter by sharing the weight of my burden. The pain remained mine alone to carry.

The girl with the spear growled, bringing me back to the present. My grip on the young defender's spear slipped. Nearby shouts told me more of the enemy would come to her aid soon.

No metal blade capped the shaft. It was nothing more than a sharpened stick. The point was still white and bright from fresh whittling. I got a good look as the point hovered in front of my face.

The child could have stabbed me through the eyes. Instead, she slashed the air, attempting to threaten me. I grabbed the spear again and wrenched the weapon from her grasp.

I lunged and the tips of my fingers brushed her head. I used to read to my daughter at bedtime. It came to me that her name was August. Later, when I was drafted, I missed her transition from an illiterate toddler to a child who loved books. Then, suddenly, she didn't want me to read to her anymore.

One day, I came home on leave, eager to return to something that felt like normal. Instead, August couldn't wait to read to me. The stories were rudimentary, but she was so proud of her new skill. As I sat beside her on her bed, she struggled through a little book about a family of bears who lived in Chicago.

I stroked August's hair as she made her way through the bear family's sweet and harmless adventures. The war was just beginning then, but I was already losing my life. The apocalypse started slow, but as with many such cataclysms throughout history, when the fall came, it seemed to happen all at once. *Q, R, S, T,* we called it. *Quarreling. Revolution. Secession. Turmoil.*

The nation's battle lines were only digital and spoken, at first. As the disease pushed us further down the road to perdition, one side jeered: *A, B, C, D. Always Be Closing Down.*

The riposte from the coastal elites was that *A, B, C, D* meant *Always Backing Chaotic Defiance.*

And the twain never met again.

I am weak, I thought. *Memory makes me weak.*

The pigtailed girl shrieked as I grabbed her hair, yanked her back, and threw her to the ground.

Looming over the child, I thought, *You are not August. You are not May. They are burnt and you are leftovers.*

Something sharp hit me from behind with great force. Somehow, I stayed on my feet. Looking down absently, I was surprised to find a spear point poking out of my chest. It was smeared with blood. I didn't know I had any of that left.

With great effort, I turned to confront my attacker. A woman, as fierce as she was small, glared at me. Her voice was low, even, and threatening. "Keep away from my child, monster."

Monster? No, I thought. *I'm no monster. I'm just like you. I am what Nature made.*

A man holding a claw hammer in each hand ran up to stand beside the girl, "Get out of there, Margaret! This thing is chock-full of the corruption!"

I heard the child scramble off to safety and turned in time to see my prey escape.

"He's a big one," the man said.

"What are you waiting for, Charlie?" the woman yelled. "Take him down! He tried to kill Margie!"

No, I thought. *I didn't want to kill your daughter. I'm just an animal now like any other. We all gotta eat. It's not personal. It's the cost of doing business.*

More of the enemy circled me. The spear still protruded from my chest, but the survival instinct is strong. I lashed out and knocked a young man to the ground. I might have tackled and bitten him, but someone grabbed the shaft of the spear at my back while another hit me from behind.

Standing amid them, the humans hit me again and again on my head, neck, and torso. I dropped to my knees and they kept going. Blunt force trauma dulled my senses, but it was a dirk at the base of my skull that finally allowed me to lie down and cease my terrible search. My hunting days were over.

I'd been mistaken from the time I was infected until that moment. My squad and I had been driven first by disease and then a deep, aching undeniable hunger. The survivors of the plague had never been our enemies, and I wasn't a soldier anymore. I hadn't been a soldier in a long time. I was just a hungry animal. Maybe that's all I'd ever been.

The Last War on Earth offered one strange beauty. I had become too numb for hate or fear. I once knew the acid taste of disgust and the torment of pain. Those tortures no longer held power over me.

They surrounded me, staring in disgust and wonder. As I lay at their feet, no feelings of defeat hindered me. As a black curtain slipped over the last of my meager consciousness, I wondered how many of my murderers envied my surprising placidity. By losing the battle for survival, I won the prize: the eternal calm of the unfettered. My last thought was how relieved I was to stop trying.

If I had still possessed the power of speech, I would have offered my liberators a benediction. "The dead are free. Thank you."

PLANTED SEEDS

Frederico knocked on his supervisor's door and poked his head in. "Cal? That cousin I was telling you about made it through the protesters. Did you want to meet him now?"

Cal Friendly took off his glasses, tossed them on his desk, and waved Frederico forward with the air of an important man ceding time to a trivial task. "I've got one minute."

Frederico ushered his cousin into the office, a space so small that the three large men's bodies took up most of the available space. "Cal, this is Raydon. Raydon, meet the boss."

Cal looked the men up and down. "Raydon? Unusual name."

"Yup!" the big man nodded. "You know the gas? Radon? It's poisonous. The stuff seeped up from my uncle's basement and gave him lung cancer. Mama hated Uncle Jimmy, so that's how I got my name. Most people just call me Ray, though. When I was in school, I liked being called Raydon because I thought it made me sound like I was from outer space. Maybe I should go back to Raydon, especially now, since the comet — "

The supervisor let out a sigh and held up a palm, cutting Ray off. "It wasn't a comet. It was a meteor. A lot of people keep calling it a comet while the rest call it a hoax. I don't know why. Aren't things complicated enough of late?"

The distant chants of protesters in the street grew louder for a moment. The words were not clear, but the mood was definitely angry.

"Did you have trouble getting through that bunch?" Cal asked.

"I'm a big guy. Nobody bothers me much."

"I'm asking if the security I hired is doing his job."

"Oh, the deputy? He asked for my ID, but it's not like he escorted me through or anything. He just pointed me to the gate, and Frederico let me in. Lotta angry people out there."

"Good enough," Cal replied. "I was going to hire private security, but an off-duty cop might get more respect because of the uniform. Not sure. They're a bunch of nuts. This business hasn't changed in a thousand years, and suddenly everyone has lost their jeezly mind!"

"Times are spooky," Frederico agreed.

"My life has been threatened. My *family's* lives have been threatened," Cal complained.

"Given who those people say they are," Ray said, "that's some special kind of ironic, huh?"

Frederico nodded. "Downright paradoxical."

"Your cousin filled you in about the job?" Cal asked.

Ray bobbed his head. "He did. But I got one question. Why not just use a backhoe?"

"I would if I could find one. Since the government declared this a national humanitarian crisis, there's not a backhoe to rent or own on this entire continent. They are all in a mad rush with the ... uh, effort."

Frederico gave Ray a smile. "What the boss is not saying is nobody can decide whether to call this a rescue or something else? The folks out there yelling in the street call it murder."

Cal rapped his desk with his knuckles. "Maybe there's doubt in your mind, Freddy, but corporate's stated policy is we're on a mission of mercy. Raydon? You squeamish?"

"For the right money, I won't be."

"No hazard pay, but I am paying double overtime all the time."

"That's the right money."

Cal pointed to the door. "Then get to it. Freddy will show you the ropes. I'm going to see if I can get corporate to authorize more security for us. We've got a lot of real estate, and there have been incidents at other locations. If someone tries to come onto our property and shut you down, call over the deputy or send them to me. We are going to do this in a tip-top and orderly fashion."

Frederico echoed, "Tip-top and orderly. Yessir!"

Once they were outside the building, Ray turned to Frederico. "What was all that 'yes, sir' shit? Did I sign up for the military? And since when do you tolerate anyone calling you Freddy?"

"Since the meteor, man. With the change in pay, this suddenly got to be a decent job. I didn't feel the same last week, but now I want to hold on to it."

"For a guy named Friendly, Cal sure doesn't live up to his name."

"Dude's under a lot of stress, man. Cut him some slack. You're on the Misericordia Memorial Gardens train now. Gotta fly the flag like a good company man. Before this is over, we'll be able to afford a house, especially when the federal money comes in. Congratulations! You're a frontline worker now."

"Gravedigger sounds like it's the opposite of frontline."

"The digging is hard, but it's also the easy part." Frederico showed his cousin to an outbuilding where they slipped into green coveralls, gloves, and masks.

Frederico pointed to a pegboard where an array of gardening tools, picks, and spades hung. "Choose your weapon, Cuz."

Ray lifted a heavy pick and a spade from their places on the wall. "This do?"

Frederico chose another shovel. Then he picked up a length of rebar from where it lay on the floor. "For the hard part," he added.

"What did Friendly mean about incidents at other locations?" Ray asked.

"One morgue and three more hospitals across Idaho had trouble just this morning."

Ray wiped his sweaty brow with his sleeve. "Shit, huh?"

"Somebody wasn't careful," Frederico replied. "The morgues, that was probably just carelessness. At the hospitals, different story. It's the families getting in the way."

Ray nodded toward the protesters marching in a circle at the front gate. "Folks like that getting in the way?"

"Exactly like that."

As they crossed the green lawn in front of the garage where the hearses were parked, some protestors spotted the pair and began a new chant. "Pro-life! Pro-life! Pro-life!"

A woman dressed entirely in black spat through the wrought iron fence. "I want to see my daddy, you bastards!" She held a placard high that read: Liberate the Undead! Grieving families need grieve no more!

Another read in big red letters: *RESURRECTION! REPENT SINNERS!*

As more protesters screamed obscenities at Ray and Frederico, they spotted various hand-lettered signs. One old woman held one that read: *Our land, our loved ones.* She screeched, "Bring my husband back to me!"

A young man pointed at the gravediggers through the fence, "Do not defy God's will, murderers!"

"There they are, Moscow, Idaho's brain trust. Lord help us. Keep walkin', Cuz, and do not engage the crazy," Frederico advised. "We aren't here to negotiate, and they aren't really in a mood to be convinced of anything."

"Gotcha."

Frederico stopped at a grave and checked his notes. The other graves nearby were mounds of freshly turned soil. "Glad you're here, Ray. Since the last guy quit, I've been doing it all myself. There's a lot of pressure from the company brass to get this done faster, but hey, I'm only one man."

Ray crouched to examine the tombstone. The granite read: *Marjorie Whedon Malloy, beloved daughter, mother, and wife.*

"Jeez! The dearly departed passed last March!"

"Yeah, huh? Buried this one myself. Big funeral, as I recall. I remember because we had a new guy named Rory. He wanted to hurry up and catch a Vandals game, so he rushed pulling up the green carpet. The mourners weren't all gone quite yet. I think it was the daughter who looked back and saw him reaching for the shovel. When love turns to grief, it's a helluva thing, man. She made a hell of a racket. Her brothers almost had to carry her off, poor woman. I feel so bad for the families. I tell everybody, life is for the living and breathing. Enjoy it while you can."

"What happened to Rory?"

"For grabbing the shovel within sight of the mourners? Got a reprimand in his file. No big thing, really. Rory stuck around until … well, here you are, taking his place."

Ray dropped his pick and shovel, got down on his hands and knees, and put his ear to the ground. "I don't hear anything."

"You will. Once you do, it'll be something you never forget."

"What's it like? I mean, for them?"

"They don't cry exactly, but you get the feeling they would if they could. Some make a lot of noise. It's the inside of the coffin that tells the tale."

"I don't get you."

"They tear at it. Fingernails get torn off. They claw through the satin straight up to the lids. Just like getting buried alive, I guess."

"Only they're dead."

"Yeah, but not *dead* dead. Not dead enough."

Ray shivered. "You're giving me the heebie-jeebies."

Frederico leaned on his shovel and whispered, "Take it easy. Back in Michigan, my first job was in a slaughterhouse. It's basically the same job. You're in the meatpacking business now. Try not to think of them as people. They're *former* people. Wherever these poor souls go, they're not here anymore."

Ray shook his head. "Cold comfort, man. *I'm* meat. I don't wanna be meat. This whole gig is a constant reminder we're all going down."

"All you can do is enjoy your time — "

"Here? Next to a funeral home and standing in a cemetery? Really?"

Frederico stepped closer to speak in a conspiratorial tone. "You gotta look to the bright side and enjoy the little things. Let me cheer you up. Last month, we had this funeral, right? Old guy dies. Cal's in the middle of embalming the old fella when the widow trots in with a special request. You know that during the embalming process, they use a butt plug?"

Ray straightened. "Say what, now?"

"A butt plug. Keep the gasses and liquids in."

"Oh, *God!* This happens to everybody? I don't wanna — "

"Cuz! Chill and keep your voice down. Check this out, though. The widow reaches into her purse and pulls out a butt plug like you get at a sex shop, right? She kisses it and says it was her husband's favorite."

"Kisses it? *Really?*"

"It's some electric doohickey called an ecstasy buzzer or some shit. She wants Cal to use that instead. That way, she can hold the remote during the funeral service and give him one last buzz."

"I'm gonna be sick."

Frederico shrugged. "I don't know. I think her intentions were actually kind of sweet. Big meaningful send-off. That's not the capper, though!"

Ray rolled his eyes. "It gets worse?"

Frederico broke into a broad grin. "Cal explains they got rules, and a regular old butt plug is not regulation. The plugs funeral directors use kinda screw in, and Cal doesn't want to risk any leakage."

"It got worse."

"Not yet. So the widow perks up and says, 'So the problem is his butt plug is too small?' This sweet little old grandma reaches into her handbag and pulls out the biggest dildo you've ever seen and says, 'This was his second favorite. Would this do?'"

The cousins had to control themselves in front of the onlookers, but the pair shook with barely contained laughter for a few minutes before setting to work.

Ray was still shaking his head as he took his first swing with his pick. "What have you gotten me into?"

"Gotta keep your spirits up in this business. Next time you're at a party, talk to the cops, the paramedics, and the funeral directors. They've got the best stories. Gallows humor delivers."

"If you say so. After a day of this, though, I'm gonna need to get myself home, have a drink, and watch some sweet and wholesome family-type show with my kids. I like stories where you know everything is going to work out okay and nobody gets hurt. I'm never going to watch a horror movie again. We're in one now."

"I resonate with your vibration, Cuz. Take your reality antidote wherever you can find it."

Someone from the street realized they were digging and let out a war cry. At that, fresh chants went up. "Death, thou shalt die! Death, thou shalt die!"

Ray shot Frederico a look. "It means so much more when they talk old-timey, huh?"

A news van pulled up, edging closer to the front gate as the driver honked the horn. The crowd parted so the vehicle could park up against the fence. A few minutes later, a cameraman stood on the vehicle's roof and set up a tripod to get an unencumbered view of the cemetery.

Frederico cursed under his breath. "Where is that deputy? Did he go for donuts or what? What's Cal paying him for?"

As the cameraman recorded them at their work, Ray paused to survey the crowd. The chants became louder. The swearing and threats of violence ramped up, too.

"I did like you said and parked a few blocks away," Ray told Frederico. "I'm thinking that when we clock out tonight, we sneak out somehow and make sure nobody follows us home. I need this job, but I don't need any hassles."

Frederico agreed. "Stick with me and we'll be set. And hey, you didn't eat breakfast this morning, did you?"

"You told me not to," Ray said.

"Glad you listened. That's how we're gonna get through this. I'm not gonna lie, it will be an ordeal, but it's like ripping off a band-aid. It'll be over quick."

A shirtless man wearing a baseball cap, jeans, and a huge tattoo of a cross on his chest climbed up on a car hood and screamed into a bullhorn to rally the crowd.

"Oh, man. Here we go," Frederico muttered. "That asshole again."

The shirtless man shouted, "These so-called people are desecrating graves and defying God's will! Who but God could send a comet to raise the dead? People don't have that power! Scientists don't have that power! The Devil doesn't have that power! But the Devil tried to defy God's might!"

Ray sighed. "How does it feel to be a so-called person serving the Devil? I grew up Southern Baptist. My pastor is gonna be pissed at this sad turn."

"I knew we should have waited for the tent. I'd rather poop in public than do this job with an audience." Frederico explained that the company had used a tent so gravediggers could work in the rain. It had been cut to pieces a few nights previously. Frederico had set up a tarp on a makeshift clothesline to screen their digs from the street, but that, too, had been vandalized the night before.

The protest leader yelled again to the approving crowd, "Jesus raised Lazarus! Only *He* can do that!"

"Shit, man. Do you think he even knows he's got a bullhorn in his hand? He should really let it do some of the work before he screams himself hoarse. You know the meteor could just be a coincidence? Nobody really knows how this started. All anybody can say for sure is everybody's thinking has turned morbid, and church attendance is *way* up."

Frederico waved his cousin back to the gravesite. "You're thinking too much."

"More than them, sure."

"Keep goin' and don't look their way," Frederico instructed. "You don't want to encourage them."

"What's their game, though? Suppose they get their way and bring their daddy and mama home. Then what?"

"Honestly? I've asked myself that same question."

"And?"

"I don't think they've thought it through that far. All they are thinking about is their own grief. That first few days after the meteor? It was a shit show, man. The morgues, hospitals, and funeral homes were alive with the dead, but it was worse around here. Soon as word got out, we had families showing up with shovels, eager to dig up their grandpa. Cal dealt with the worst of it. Everybody was threatening to sue while he tried to quote health and safety regulations at them. It was only the public safety decrees from the governor and the president that made the protesters step back and take a breath. The National Guard was here the first week."

"And now where are they?"

Frederico shrugged. "Keep it under your hat. The secret they don't want anyone to know is that the army is spread too thin to be much help. They can't be everywhere. Even if they were, what are they really going to do? Fix bayonets and create more of the rampaging undead?"

Ray wiped his sweaty brow with his sleeve. "Solid point. Sounds like if those protesters figure that detail out, we're in trouble. This gig might not pay enough, after all."

Frederico smiled. "Keep digging and complain to me later when you're buying yourself a new Tesla. It's a good salary, plenty of fresh air until we hit the stink, and you get paid to exercise. A few months here, and you'll get more muscles and lose that extra sixty pounds of spare tire you've been complaining about for years."

Ray shot him a hard look. "Forty pounds."

"Sweat sixty pounds off, and you'll be tip-top like me."

Ray cursed his cousin, suggesting Frederico perform an act upon himself that was both obscene and physically impossible.

"Hey, hey! No cursing in front of the Lazarus. Respect!"

"Speakin' of respect, shouldn't a minister be present to help us send her on her way? Isn't there a ceremony? Seems like there should be."

"This is a temporary disinterment, so, no. They already got one funeral. Corporate briefly contemplated charging the families for a second funeral. That's when the first real riots hit. Glad we aren't doing that. The logistics are tough enough. Our job is simple now: Put a stake through their heads and tuck them back into bed."

"Through the heart won't do, huh?"

"Think zombies, not vampires."

"So not even a single clergyman on duty?"

Frederico nodded. "Given the suffering of all those trapped, we don't have time to get all sentimental. We got a lot of graves to dig up and cover over again. Besides, bulldozers, backhoes, and clergy are all busy elsewhere and everywhere. Do you know how many graves there are in this country? The president made Arlington Cemetery the country's first priority and that sucked up all the digging equipment for four states."

"So ... when you do it, do you say a few words?"

Frederico shook his head. "You'll see when we get to it, it's kind of a frenzied moment. No time to choose your words. Pray after if you want. Me? I just try to get it over with quick as I can and move on to the next. At the end of the day, I have a very long, hot shower."

Ray stopped abruptly. "Did you hear that?"

A soft pounding emanated from beneath their feet.

"That's Mrs. Malloy. She heard us. Hang on, honey. We're a-comin'!"

"Didn't think we'd get to her so fast. Doesn't seem deep enough."

"Some places, six feet is the rule. In Idaho, the regulation states the grave space is just five."

As they dug, Ray chattered nervously, "Did you hear about what happened in Seattle? A couple of kids dug up Bruce Lee's grave. Thought they'd resurrect their hero."

"Same thing happened at Graceland, trying to bring Elvis back. The fans were disappointed. Whoever's in charge of figuring out this shit says the meteor's effect only works on fresher bodies. No word on the oldest Lazarus yet."

"The head of the CDC was on the news this morning. She doesn't call them that. The preferred term for the resurrected is 'post-humans.' You know? Like posthumous?"

Frederico glanced over his shoulder at the angry crowd. "Maybe not a bad idea, but I hate puns."

More protesters arrived along with another deputy. This one had a whistle and wasn't afraid to use it. After a few minutes of confusion, it became clear the new arrivals were counter-protesters. Panting from exertion, Ray took a break and read out the signs they carried to Frederico. "This one says 'In Heaven or in Hell, but not here.' And that one says 'It is an abomination, not life.'"

Frederico muttered, "Sounds like another religious contingent has arrived, but they're okay with what we're doing. The news doesn't pay much attention to them. They might even outnumber the ones who want to take the resurrected home, but you'd never know it from the mainstream media."

"If another riot breaks out, and they beat each other over the head with their signs, that'll get the word out," Ray replied.

Even more counter-protesters arrived. This group wore white lab coats and Halloween costumes that looked like cheap imitations of Hazmat suits.

Frederico paused his digging to survey the growing crowd. "That'll be kids from the university, no doubt. When the science people and the religious people are in agreement — "

"It's really going to rile up the half-naked guy with the bull-horn," Ray finished for him. "A couple of deputies aren't gonna do it, Cuz. We should stop until we can put a screen up. They're freakin' out."

"Eyes on the prize, Ray. It's your first day. Let's make a good first impression so you have a second day, okay?"

Ray sighed and picked up his spade again. As they dug, the noises from within the coffin became louder.

"Sounds like somebody's strangling a cat in there," Ray muttered.

"Restless Coffin Syndrome. Maintain course and speed until I tell you."

The pair kept digging. The pounding from within the box got louder.

"Mrs. Malloy's bouncing around in there like a june bug in a bottle."

Frederico grabbed Ray's arm and ordered him to stop. "This is the tricky part." He pointed to a short ladder laying in the grass nearby. "Put that on the lid and put your weight on it while I clear the last of the dirt away."

"Why?"

"You ever have a jack-in-the-box when you were a kid?"

"Yeah."

"You don't want a repeat of that here."

"I can dig it."

"Was that a pun?"

"Could be."

"What'd I say about puns?"

Ray placed the ladder atop the coffin lid and leaned hard. "I got Mrs. Malloy locked down. In the future, they're going to have to start making caskets with locks on them."

"Cal tells me that's already in the works. Cremations are up 300%, but the cost of turning bodies to ash is shooting up 1000%. People are generally slow on the uptake, but capitalism adjusts pretty quick when there's an ugly situation to exploit."

"Deep. Can you do the thing, please? I'm getting nervous over here, and I'm gonna need a pee break soon. Also, if this thing goes south, I might shit my pants."

"First time is always the hardest, virgin. I'm up on this now, so don't panic and you'll be safe."

"What? I thought I was already safe!"

"Rory thought he was safe, too. He panicked."

"You said he quit."

"He did, in the ambulance on the way to the hospital, right after he got bit."

"Son of a bitch."

"You needed the job. I got you the job. Capitalism, baby."

"We're gonna have a long talk after this."

"Just say thank you. No need for more." Frederico pulled the length of rebar from his belt as he straddled the open grave.

"What's the plan?" Ray asked nervously.

"Not much to the plan. As you take the weight off the lid, I'll lift it up and jam this chunk o' metal through her skull. Some say to go through the ear or the eye, but I'll drop down, use my weight and gravity so there's no fussy aiming involved, just brute force. Ready?"

"No."

"Time to pop your cherry, Cuz!"

"There's gotta be a better way to do this."

"You'll be the one holding the rebar next time."

"What?"

"You heard me. Now, ready?"

"No!"

"Steady ... go!"

Ray pulled the ladder away as the coffin lid burst open. Marjorie Malloy had been a school teacher from Post Falls. She moved to Moscow right out of school and taught elementary school for eleven years before getting hit by a truck. She lingered on the edge of death for days before tipping over life's cliff and succumbing to her injuries. Now that she was back, feral and growling as she scrambled to her feet, she was almost unrecognizable as having once been human.

Frederico dropped onto her. He drove the length of rebar into the corpse but missed the skull. The metal sank deep into the depression under her right collarbone.

"Too slow with the ladder, man! You gotta commit!" Frederico complained.

The stench that rose from her rotting corpse drove Ray to his knees. Clutching his stomach, he yanked down his mask just in time to projectile vomit into his cousin's face.

Blinded and not daring to wipe the vomit from his face, Frederico cursed as he struggled to withdraw the rebar. Gore made his gloved hand slick and the rebar was stuck.

Ray coughed and sputtered as the post-human clawed at the sleeves of Frederico's coveralls. Ray managed to catch his breath long enough to apologize. "Sorry, man! I didn't want to go the whole day without food, so ... huevos rancheros!"

"Help me!" Frederico begged just before he threw up into his mask.

Marjorie Malloy slipped from Frederico's grasp and turned. At first, it appeared she was climbing him like a tree. Then she sank her teeth into his nose and whipped her head back and forth, peeling the cartilage from his face.

Frederico screamed.

Ray threw up a little more and then clutched his groin as the dry heaves set in.

Marjorie Malloy went back for more, tearing away the eyelid and the skin from above Frederico's left eye.

Frederico continued screaming as the mob of protesters cheered.

The bare-chested man with the bullhorn yelled something about divine retribution as a Catholic priest rushed forward to pull the man down from his pulpit atop a car hood. The men argued but were soon pulled apart.

Two young men and a woman climbed atop the news van and dropped over the fence to rush to the gravediggers' aid.

The woman in the white coat arrived first. "I'm a doctor! Where are you hurt?"

Still on his hands and knees and shaking, Ray pointed at the post-human devouring his cousin's face. "Help him!"

The two men who followed the doctor skidded to a stop beside the open grave and paled in fright. One of the men turned to the other would-be rescuers. "Holy feeding frenzy. I'm not getting in there. This is a job for Animal Control."

"Or an exorcist," the other man agreed.

Frederico had slid halfway into the coffin with Marjorie Malloy on top of him. A gout of blood shot up from a torn artery in Frederico's neck.

"Oh, God!" Ray cried.

"God's got nothing to do with this." In shock, the doctor stared. "She was human once. I don't care how those religious fanatics dress it up. She's gone full-blown piranha."

Frederico yelled in pain, but his cries were muffled and getting weaker.

"Get away from there," the doctor told Ray.

"I can't just leave him! He's my cousin! I'll get her, you pull him out."

All three would-be rescuers shook their heads. The woman said, "Don't — "

The zombie stopped abruptly, turned, and pulled one of the men into the grave. The man reached out to his friend to be pulled up, but the corpse of Marjorie Malloy sank its teeth into his left wrist.

His friend, the doctor, and Ray backed away in horror. "Too late," Ray said. "Too damn late."

From the view of the camera atop the news van, viewers across the nation and eventually the world watched as Ray and the remaining two would-be rescuers cringed and backed away from the open grave. A moment later, the trio rushed back toward the fence. Unable to climb the wrought iron fence, they sprinted for the gate. Finding that exit locked and blocked by cheering protesters, they ran to the funeral home and whipped the doors open to escape inside.

Minutes passed as the mob erupted into pandemonium. A news reporter tried to speak to the camera but was drowned out by the cheers and screams of the protesters and counter-protesters.

The bare-chested man began to climb atop the news van, but the Catholic priest pulled him down from the ladder. They argued again with increasing vehemence. The news camera did not capture that moment, but at least a dozen camera phones recorded the priest yanking the bullhorn from his opponent's grasp and bludgeoning him with it. The bare-chested man fell to the pavement, grabbing at his bloodied face. Amid cheers and boos, the priest climbed the ladder to stand atop the van, nudging the cameraman aside.

"Shut up!" the priest yelled. He pulled off his collar, perhaps in an effort to avoid being identified. (It was far too late for that, and days later, he was called to Rome for what was described as a stern discussion with the pope.) "Hush, all of you! Hush and listen!"

And, just for a moment, the crowd — both pro and con — went quiet.

Taken by surprise at his sudden platform, the priest opened his mouth to speak. No one was interested in what he might say. The growls, howls, and screams emanating from Misericordia Memorial Gardens proved far too distracting and much more interesting.

Frederico Perez and a man later identified as Brent Hatt, a premed student, emerged from the grave. Wounded, battered, and covered in blood, they staggered toward the crowd.

The mob stood in stunned silence for a few beats as the newly made post-humans looked around as if they'd just arrived on the planet. That was a point many conspiracy theorists picked up on, suggesting those raised from the dead had actually been taken over by aliens.

Then the beings once known as Frederico Perez and Brent Hatt charged the fence. It was the deputies' turn to earn their pay. The police unloaded their weapons on the pair, hitting each man only a couple of times. When that had no effect, with trembling hands, the deputies reloaded. It was only when the zombies came up to the wrought iron fence, growling and drooling, that they could put the muzzles of their pistols against each post-human's forehead and truly end them.

Numerous radio, TV, and podcast hosts of a certain bias focused on that moment and posed another untestable hypothesis. "Everything was new to them because they were reborn! These aren't zombies. They're babies! They aren't our enemies. Who would be so insensitive as to call the late Marjorie Malloy a beast? She's a baby! And the government has that poor woman chained up in some lab somewhere."

Others asked, "What terrible experiments are government scientists performing on her body, this child of God? This new Lazarus!"

The commentators were less concerned for the poor dead gravedigger and the student from the University of Idaho. They weren't coming back. However, many broadcasters did make hay out of the fact that only bullets to the head could erase them. "Nigh immortal!" they crowed. "Truly, these are blessed and misunderstood beings sent by a higher power! When they recover, they can tell us what heaven is like! What person do you know who can withstand multiple gunshot wounds and not even flinch? What medical secrets might lurk within these powerful people? What a miracle and a gift these folks are! And what is the government really doing with their bodies? Turning these holy vessels into super soldiers, that's what!"

Though the nation and the world were divided on whether Frederico and Brent were gifts from God, an unhappy cosmic accident, or an unholy abomination, all sides agreed on one point. Everyone was certain governments around the world would try to figure out how to use post-humans to fight wars. Some used that argument to affirm that they should all be destroyed. Many took that same information as confirmation that post-humans should be preserved so no military advantage could be ceded. And lots of people wanted to unlock the zombies' secrets so they, too, could be "nigh immortal."

Frederico and Brent's last names were soon forgotten. They became little more than a footnote. But everyone remembered Marjorie Malloy's appearance as she crawled up from what was supposed to be her place of eternal rest. Covered in gore, she moved awkwardly and slowly. "Like a spider with one broken leg," a newscaster on the scene commented.

She made her way to the fence and growled at the protesters. She was in such a state of decomposition, the deputies did not raise their weapons. Their pistols hung by their sides as they stared at her in awe.

The bare-chested man fell to his knees in prayer. In a long, rambling, and loud speech, he thanked God for delivering his wife back to him. "Sent back from Death Itself!" he proclaimed.

Others who shared his faith also fell to their knees while others stood and watched in horror, taking pictures of the growling beast lunging through the fence bars, eager to feed and make more of her kind.

It was later revealed that the bare-chested man, Benjamin Ross, was no relation whatsoever to Marjorie Malloy. However, the lie was more compelling to viewers than the truth. Where his detractors saw an opportunist, those of his ilk saw a grieving husband and a chance at eternal love renewed. His Kickstarter campaign was first used to bail him out of jail for drunk and disorderly conduct. In the minds of his fans, he was a tragic and romantic figure, a victim of uncaring authorities.

Ross, claiming religious persecution, raised hundreds of thousands of dollars for the legal fight to save Marjorie Malloy from extermination. She perished in government custody under mysterious circumstances which only fed her legend.

Even after the government admitted she had been destroyed for attacking a researcher, Benjamin Ross claimed she was alive, and he needed more funds to free and care for her while the couple endured a course of recovery. The last anyone had heard, Ross took the millions donated to him to Costa Rica to live in a seaside mansion.

But that's not the end of the story. Two days after Marjorie Malloy escaped the grave, Cal Friendly stood behind a podium in front of Misericordia Memorial Gardens. Beside him, in a business suit concealing body armor, the governor of Idaho sweated copiously.

News services from around the world had converged on Moscow. The phenomenon was global, and there had been many other incidents, but opposing forces on both sides had gathered to march and hold candlelight vigils. The small city was under curfew as the National Guard patrolled the streets. The media knew where conflict was most likely to erupt, so the world watched as Cal Friendly stepped into the unforgiving heat of the spotlight.

Cal blew on the microphone, tapped the device to make sure it was working, and cleared his throat nervously. He did not look up at the crowd or into the camera. Instead, he read his speech from cards dictated to him by his corporate overlords.

"Madame Governor, ladies and gentlemen of the press, and to the general public to whom we have opened our gates this sad day. I'm also opening my heart to you all. In the past few days, I've had some time to look back on my mistakes. With the clarity of sober second thought, I now see how we ... uh ... tripped up. When faced with a crisis and a mystery, it's natural and expected that errors will be made even among people acting with only the best of intentions."

Discontented murmurs rippled through the crowd. What had first been called the Lazarus Plague had been reframed and transformed by public opinion. Now, even the most thoughtful news commentators referred to the disaster as the Lazarus Debate. People from all sides of that debate were present and restless.

"We have lost valued employees and we mourn them," Cal continued. "In response to this crisis, we will be enacting new policies and safety protocols."

In a dramatic moment he'd practiced in front of a mirror many times the night before, Cal pointed to the Misericordia Memorial Gardens beyond the assembled. "You have no doubt seen recordings of many so-called Lazarus people in hospitals and morgues."

At the use of the word so-called, several people booed and pushed their way forward to the front of the crowd. The governor subtly stepped away from Cal and edged closer to her bodyguards.

Cal continued, "What concerns me, and all the fine people who have served Memorial Gardens Funeral Home franchises for more than a generation, are the people in our care. We have always treated your loved ones with the utmost respect."

"Tell the truth, you ghoul!" an agitated man at the back cried.

"And love!" Cal exclaimed. "A deep and abiding love ... you know ... like good caretakers!"

More murmurs of disapproval rippled through the crowd which only served to increase Cal's anxiety. "B-by love," he stammered, "I-I d-don't mean anything s-sexual."

Having unwittingly introduced dark suspicions, even among his supporters, Cal was met by even more boos. Struggling to compose himself, he wiped his brow and struggled on with an appeal to the crowd's sympathy. "This situation is not our fault! No one could have anticipated ... w-we're getting sued by the families of our employees and quite a few families of the dead."

"Good, ya greedy heathen!" the agitated man crowed.

Across the world, translators working on the live broadcast informed their viewers that Cal was a greedy non-believer.

"Our loved ones have come back!" a woman screamed. "They're back and they're immortal!"

"I still think it's aliens," a man at the edge of the crowd added. "It's cool. I vote we let the Lazarus People live and let live, you know? We don't want to piss off the aliens. I mean, the people coming back, they're like space emissaries, right?"

To Cal's alarm, several people in the gathering nodded sagely at this latest salvo. He could see he wasn't just losing the crowd. He'd never had them. Cal tried the move in the mirror again since it had gone over so well with his wife and kids during rehearsals. "Out there, in those many graves, there are people, if they haven't decayed too much, who are clawing at the upholstery, trying to free themselves from their prisons. They are trapped and it would seem, in some distress."

He immediately realized that qualifying the level of their distress was a public relations error. Some in the crowd began swearing imaginatively and made vile threats about burying him alive "to see how he'd like it."

"They are in terrible distress," Cal said, "torture even. From now on, all Misericordia Memorial Gardens franchises will adopt new measures to ensure the improved safety of our employees and to return all our cemeteries to what they are meant to be. Graves should be a place of rest and for remembrance, a sweet retreat for quiet contemplation of life's mysteries."

The CNN correspondent could contain himself no longer. "What new measures, Mr. Friendly?"

"We used metal ... um ... implements to ... you know ... set things right. Back to normal, I mean. From now on, *three* employees will be assigned to each disinterment to return our guests to their eternal rest. Given the sober, caring, and quiet nature of our work and the setting, we did not feel the use of firearms on our properties was the correct course. In light of recent events, we've reconsidered."

The agitated man who had heckled from the rear of the crowd rushed the stage. "You're gonna shoot my son in the head? You first!"

He drew a small pistol and got off four shots before the governor's bodyguards returned fire. The guard shot the attacker in the chest and wounded a Fox News sound technician.

Though every shot missed him, and the funeral director was unharmed, Cal Friendly was furious. He jumped down from the little stage and marched over to the man who tried to murder him on international television. Without hesitation, Cal scooped up the dead man's pistol and fired the rest of the clip into the corpse's forehead. The body shook with each round, and Cal only stopped when the pistol clicked empty.

Tossing the weapon atop the dead man, Cal came up close to the camera and stared out at the world as if speaking to each viewer directly. With heat and venom, he snarled, "And that's how it's done, motherfuckers."

The bodyguards had the presence of mind to scoot Cal and the governor away before those who disagreed tore them apart. It was unfortunate the funeral director swore. His detractors never failed to bring up his understandable use of profanity in the debate that ensued.

Congress debated. The Supreme Court eventually made rulings about when, where, and how it was deemed acceptable to take what they called "anti-life measures."

That's how we became the Divided States of America. We aren't special in that way. Everybody had differing opinions because, living people being what they are, emotions run high everywhere. That often derailed civilized debate and rational thought.

We don't call them Lazarus People, as some still do. It's kind of funny, isn't it? The outbreaks just grew and grew as we humans debated ourselves close to extinction. It's only the post-humans that are united. All they want to do is eat us. Their side doesn't have any debate. They do make great soldiers, but they only serve one mission, and that's to fill their stomachs.

"Aw, jeez, Ray, you're scaring them with your stories, and the things you say are not age-appropriate!"

"What's age-appropriate has changed. Every young survivor gets a very short childhood now, Boo-Boo! We don't have TV or school anymore. I'm just telling the story, boosting morale, and filling in the gaps — "

"Didn't you hear me? You are *scaring* them! I'm more concerned with your morals than I am with their morale. You've gone a little crazy since — "

"The girls are twelve, thirteen, and eleven. We can't shelter them forever. I'm *preparing* them. I appreciate their help with the gardening, but it's time they at least took over sentry duty. "

"I want them innocent, and here you are telling them a horror story."

"Telling them the truth. They're all innocent, but stupid and naive could get them killed ... or worse, undead."

"Do better, Ray."

"Okay, I can see by your little faces that you are worried. You needn't be. We've adapted to the new normal. I'm telling you the history of the post-humans to ease your fears, girls. You asked why we tie up your grandparents each night at bedtime and lock them in their rooms. The answer is, they are getting on in years, and we want you safe in your rooms when it's your bedtime.

"Every night, your mother and I check the locks. We've got plenty of ammunition, and we're always very careful when we go out. Someday soon, when you're a little older and can hit the bull's eye every time, you'll be able to come with us to the farmer's market.

Until then, I want you to understand that you are completely safe here."

"Thank you, Ray. That is better."

"I should add, though, that if you ever see Mommy or Daddy fall down, and we don't get up, run to the parent who *isn't* lying down right away. If that happens ... well, I guess then we'll have to show how it's done."

MORE POST-APOCALYPTIC & DYSTOPIAN FUN

This Plague of Days

What will you do to protect your family in the zombie apocalypse? Young Jaimie Spencer is an unlikely hero amid the ashes and ruins of our world. On the spectrum and selectively mute, he's more obsessed with his dictionary than with the fate of humanity. However, before this epic story is over, Good will do battle with Evil and Jaimie is our champion.

Robert's most successful series to date, *This Plague of Days* won Honorable Mention in their Self-published Ebook Awards from *Writers' Digest*.

All three seasons of this trilogy are available as an omnibus or individually as ebooks or paperbacks.

AFTER Life

Zombies will soon invade the United States. Which side will you join, the infected or the damned?

Artificial Facilitation Therapy for Enhanced Response (AFTER) was a biomimetic stem cell nanotechnology with numerous health and wellness applications. Then a military contractor weaponized it using brain parasites. When the zombie apocalypse arrives, we soon discover that genetically engineered zombies are hard to kill.

Officer Daniel Harmon is tasked with stopping the epidemic. Dr. Chloe Robinson needs to get her creation back under control. We can't always get what we want.

The *AFTER Life* trilogy is available in ebook form or in paperback.

Endemic (dropping November 2021!)

I was a nail. I am a hammer.

As the United States falls to disease, killers and thieves rule New York. Bookish, neurotic, and nerdy, Ovid Fairweather finds herself trapped in the struggle for survival.

Bullied by her father, haunted by her dead therapist, and hunted by marauders, Ovid is forced to fight.

With only the voices in her head as her guides, an unlikely heroine will become a queen.

~

Citizen Second Class

Set a decade later in the same universe as *Endemic*, Kismet is a young woman who must travel to Atlanta to find work to feed what's left of her family. The city has become a fortress for rich religious zealots who care nothing for the poor. Just below the surface, a revolution simmers as disaster looms. Join the fight.

~

Amid Mortal Words

A dangerous stranger met on a train leaves behind a powerful book. With mere words, this book could destroy the world or save it. This power is now in the hands of one man relying on a mysterious woman to guide him toward the Apocalypse or away from our destruction. It's a roller coaster ride filled with twists and turns toward a surprising conclusion that will keep you up all night reading.

~

Robot Planet

The robots are unfailingly polite until the moment they kill you. This future isn't merely a forbidding dystopia. It's cyberpunk scary. In this series of four novellas, three very different people join forces to combat the rise of the Next Intelligence. The odds are against us.

Start your next adventure by grabbing *Robot Planet, The Complete Series,* available in paperback or ebook.

~

Haunting Lessons (with Holly Pop)

This is not a ghost story. It only starts out that way.

Tamara Smith is a young woman from the Midwest who experiences an unspeakable tragedy. Soon she sees apparitions. That's only the beginning of her adventures. Running away to New York, she soon discovers a secret world of dark magic doing combat with alien forces from another dimension.

If she is to save the world from the coming invasion, Tam must train to become a leader among the Choir Invisible. She fights for us all.

Death Lessons, Fierce Lessons, and *Dream's Dark Flight* are also part of this series of gripping adventures.

~

All Empires Fall

How will the world end? In this short story collection, Robert shares several tales of the apocalypse. It comes in flood and fire. It stabs at us out of the darkness of space.

Robert Chazz Chute has lots of dark ideas for you to consider and revel in as you stay up through the night, turning pages to each ending of our world.

ALL BOOKS BY ROBERT CHAZZ CHUTE

Find links to all books by Robert Chazz Chute at

AllThatChazz.com

~ DYSTOPIAN AND APOCALYPTIC FICTION ~

This Plague of Days, Season 1

This Plague of Days, Season 2

This Plague of Days, Season 3

This Plague of Days, Omnibus Edition

THE AFTER Life TRILOGY

Inferno

Purgatory

Paradise

AFTER Life (Box Set)

Endemic

Citizen Second Class

Amid Mortal Words

Robot Planet, The Complete Series

Haunting Lessons, Book 1 of *The Dimension War*

Death Lessons, Book 2 of *The Dimension War*

ABOUT THE AUTHOR

Robert Chazz Chute is a former crime and science journalist. A winner of eight writing awards, he pens fiction full-time from Other London.

For updates, links to his books, and Patreon support of his fiction podcasts, please visit Robert at AllThatChazz.com.

www.ingramcontent.com/pod-product-compliance
Lightning Source LLC
Chambersburg PA
CBHW071405170626
46811CB00003B/1269